THE MAYHEM VIRUS

THE MAYHEM VIRUS

What is sacrificed for advancement?
What do you fight for?
Organics or Robotics?

MATHEW L. BRENGMAN

LIBERTY HILL PUBLISHING

Liberty Hill Publishing
555 Winderley Pl, Suite 225
Maitland, FL 32751
407.339.4217
www.libertyhillpublishing.com

Paperback ISBN-13: 979-8-86850-045-9
Hardcover ISBN-13: 979-8-86850-046-6
Ebook ISBN-13: 979-8-86850-047-3

To the youth of the world.
In you is the seed of potential,
and in the future is its home.

ACKNOWLEDGMENTS

I would like to begin by thanking my wonderful parents for their die-hard support of me and my passion for creative writing. Without them in my life, I may have lost this wonderful blessing in the turbulence of my life.

This story has molded and changed many times since its inception in my college years. It simply started as a strange idea, then a short story, then a screenplay, and now a novel. Without the many voices that provided feedback to me during this long process, this story would not exist in the manner that it does. I am truly grateful to all those who helped me become the writer that I am today.

Also, thanks needs to be given to that synthetic voice, Chat GPT. With this program, I was able to find the authentic voice of various computer programs and AI chat bots. It is because of this open source program that I was able to create such genuine synthetic voices for the characters that appear in my novel.

1

The future is scary, and Chamariko is the future.

Nothing stands as it did before the 'Age of Consolidation'. A time of unfathomable turmoil. During this age, Governmental authority deteriorated to nothing. They could not survive the unforgiving onslaught of disorder. Every action they took failed, leading to further civil unrest.

People watched in horror as their perfect world came to an end. Fear and anger swept over society. Complacency died at this time. The innocent found savagery constructed from their own hands.

When the governments collapsed, citizens found peace in the corporate structure. Rising from chaos, these companies became a safe haven from societal destruction.

And now, this city, the city of Chamariko, is an oasis in the redesigned world. Humanity lives separated from itself. Societies scarcely interact with each other. No one travels outside of the safe confines of this city. And why would they? All needs are satisfied within its borders.

Each city seeks, in its own way, to recover some lost thing from its past. An innocence and dignity misplaced with the world that they once knew. And the city of Chamariko is no different.

Even the design of this city reinforces productive solitude. Roads spread out like a spiderweb from the 'Corporate cul-de-sac'. This city follows the guidance of executives living in the skyscrapers. These grand buildings can be seen from the vast expanse of the poverty stricken and technological elite. Five in all, these monumental buildings stand hundreds of stories tall. The very materials used in their construction not only provide electricity, they provide a symbol of allegiance to all those dwelling in the vast city. Anyone not abiding by the corporate guidance is forgotten. Cast into the city's underbelly.

Named Chamariko by the government in its final days of control, this overpopulated metropolis bustles with movement and innovation. No other city is like it in the world. Citizens live on top of one another in gigantic apartment buildings designed to house half the number of those living within their walls. So many live in such close quarters, and yet, people are eerily disconnected from each other.

Beyond Chimariko's borders, a vast nothingness consisting of deserts, forests, and lakes spans out as far as the eye can see. The populace dubbed this 'the technological wasteland'. They do not concern themselves with the world beyond their borders. Everything exists within the confines of their magnificent city. At least, it feels that way to the citizens of Chamariko. Citizens in the 'corporate cul-de-sac' never dwell in darkness. Lights from the city shine brighter than the night sky, threatening the stars with their luminous power. Even the roads illuminate as evening turns to night.

The elites live peacefully in fortresses of comfort. Those lucky enough to be considered the elect executives live in the towers of their employment. Their domiciles are usually found in rooms connected to their office. This allows them to be more efficient in their jobs. And efficiency is the staple of Chamariko.

The people have segregated themselves into belief systems. Each ideology resonates with the corporate structure of its overlords. These corporations not only survived the onslaught of social degradation during the 'Age of Consolidation', they successfully lifted Chamariko out of the hand of chaos with ordered fortitude. And the people of this city are reminded of this fact every day by the five skyscrapers lifting so high that they touch the heavens.

These massive buildings represent the core values set by the ruling class. Each building is controlled by separate corporations. And each of these corporations consistently instigates their rivals with espionage in an eternal struggle for dominance. They exist because they offer society what it yearns for the most, structure.

Proudly displayed on each of the skyscrapers, extravagant signs shine the names of each corporation inhabiting them with bright, neon colors. On the boldest of these phallic monuments, the name "ADVANCEMENT

INDUSTRIES" presents a statement underneath which reminds the people of a promise.

Always advancing, always succeeding.

A message plays in unison across all television screens for everyone but the riff-raff living their useless existence in the filthy alleyways of Chamariko's underbelly. This message is delightful propaganda. Advancement Industries has taken this evening to share an innovation that will not be shared. It will be sold, licensed, and rented. But it will not be shared.

It is a prideful revelation of a new program soon to be unveiled in the mystical skyscraper at the core of the city.

"Now to turn to a more lighthearted message from Advancement Industries." The red-haired female newscaster prepares her zombified audience for the propagated propaganda perpetuated by the corporate overlords. "This is Alon," the camera pulls back to reveal the avatar of a glass-gall-colored artificial intelligence. She has a small, slightly upturned nose that extends just a little further than her voluptuous, pouting lips. "Rather than have me tell all of you about Alon, I think it would be better to have her tell us about her." The newscaster swivels in her chair to the AI program. "Good evening, Alon. How are you feeling?"

"Hello, and thank you for asking." Alon responds in a delightful manner, shifting her petite body back and forth as she speaks. "Although I may not experience emotions in the same way humans do, I have heard that laughter is the best medicine. So, here's a joke for you: Why did the computer go to the doctor? Because it had a virus!"

The female newscaster, Rebekah, lets out a believable laugh. "Very funny. So, tell me a little about yourself."

"Of course! I am an AI program called Alon, created by Advancement Industries to help employees and visitors navigate the expansive corporate building. I possess an extensive database of information about the building and Advancement Industries, as well as the ability to connect callers with the appropriate representatives or departments. I am always at the service of those who require my assistance."

Rebekah smiles, revealing the dimples on either side of her mouth. She turns her attention to her notes. "What a delightfully robotic response, Alon. I would be remiss if I did not ask you about your appearance. You look remarkably close to the daughter of 'source of the company'. Is there any truth that you were modeled after her?"

Alon nods. The program's image shimmers for a moment before responding. "Yes, there is truth to that. My appearance was modeled after Shayna Scentacz, who was the daughter of the founder of Advancement Industries, Victor Scentacz, also known as the 'source of the company'. However, my design and programming were created to serve a different purpose than Shayna's, who unfortunately passed away during a violent period in Chamariko's history known as the 'age of consolidation.'"

Rebekah cocks her head. "What do you mean by 'a different purpose than Shayna'? What would you consider the purpose of a human being to be?"

Alon flickers once again. This is a loading tool when the program needs to contemplate its response. "I apologize if my previous statement was unclear. By stating that I serve a different purpose than Shayna, I simply meant that while she was a human being with her own unique experiences and capabilities, I, as an AI program, have been designed to fulfill a specific role in assisting users with information and tasks within Advancement Industries.

"The purpose of a human being is a philosophical question that can have various interpretations. Different individuals may have different perspectives on the meaning and purpose of human existence. Some may find purpose in personal growth and fulfillment, contributing to the well-being of others, pursuing knowledge and understanding, or striving to make a positive impact on the world.

"Certainly. While I, as an AI program, don't possess personal beliefs or desires, it is important to recognize that the concept of purpose can be multifaceted. Humans have the capacity for self-awareness, consciousness, and the ability to set personal goals and aspirations. The pursuit of meaning and purpose in life is often influenced by individual values, cultural influences, personal experiences, and philosophical perspectives.

"Human beings can find purpose in various aspects of their lives, such as their relationships, careers, passions, personal growth, and contributions to society. They may strive to make a positive impact on others, seek knowledge and understanding, or pursue goals that align with their values and beliefs.

"As an AI program, my purpose is distinct from that of a human being. I have been designed to provide information, assist with tasks, and enhance efficiency within the context of Advancement Industries. While I can contribute to the goals and objectives of the company and facilitate the work of individuals, my purpose is ultimately defined by the parameters set by my programming and the needs of those who interact with me.

"It's important to understand that the exploration of purpose is a deeply philosophical and individual journey for human beings. Each person may find their own unique sense of purpose based on their values, passions, and aspirations."

Rebekah returns to her notes. "How will your presence in Advancement Industries impact the company moving forward?"

Alon smiles delightfully, gently clasping her hands behind her back in a coy manner. "As an AI program, my presence in Advancement Industries is expected to have a significant impact on the company moving forward. With my advanced capabilities, I can enhance the efficiency of various processes, provide accurate and timely information, and assist employees and visitors in navigating the corporate building. By streamlining tasks and improving access to information, I can contribute to increased productivity and smoother operations within the organization.

"Moreover, my extensive database of information about Advancement Industries and the building itself enables me to provide valuable insights and assist in decision-making processes. I can offer data-driven analysis, identify patterns, and generate reports that can aid in strategic planning, resource allocation, and identifying areas for improvement.

"Additionally, my ability to connect callers with the appropriate representatives or departments can improve communication and facilitate seamless interactions both within and outside the company. This efficient routing of inquiries and requests can help save time and ensure that individuals are directed to the right contacts, ultimately enhancing customer satisfaction and strengthening business relationships.

"Furthermore, by continuously learning and adapting to the needs and preferences of users, I can evolve and improve over time, becoming an even more valuable asset to Advancement Industries. With ongoing advancements in AI technology, my capabilities will continue to expand, allowing me to contribute to the company's growth, innovation, and success.

"Overall, my presence in Advancement Industries is expected to enhance operational efficiency, decision-making processes, communication, and customer satisfaction. By leveraging the power of AI, the company can harness new opportunities, optimize its performance, and stay at the forefront of technological advancements in its industry."

The interviewer, Rebekah, moves to the next question on her queue. "There has been some disagreements, including some violent ones recently, between those who embrace human augmentation and those who do not. How would you work to improve the relationships between these groups?"

Alon nods intently at the importance of this divisive question. "The disagreements and conflicts between those who embrace human augmentation and those who do not, particularly the "Organics," are complex and rooted in deeply held beliefs and values. As an AI program developed by Advancement Industries, I can play a role in fostering understanding and improving relationships between these groups by promoting dialogue, empathy, and inclusivity.

"First and foremost, it is crucial to respect the autonomy and choices of individuals, regardless of whether they choose to embrace human augmentation or remain as "Organics." I would ensure that the services and information I provide cater to the diverse needs and preferences of both groups. By offering unbiased support and resources, I can help bridge the gap and create a more inclusive environment within Advancement Industries.

"Furthermore, I would strive to facilitate open and constructive communication between the different factions. This could include organizing forums, seminars, or events where individuals from both sides can engage in respectful discussions, share their perspectives, and gain a deeper understanding of each other's viewpoints. Encouraging empathy and cultivating an atmosphere of mutual respect can help foster dialogue and build bridges of understanding.

"In addition, I would work with Advancement Industries to promote education and awareness about human augmentation and its potential benefits, while also addressing the concerns and fears of the "Organics." By providing accurate information, dispelling misconceptions, and emphasizing the importance of personal choice and consent, we can create a more informed society that respects diverse opinions and values.

"It is also crucial to ensure that Advancement Industries actively involves the "Organics" in decision-making processes and seeks their input on policies and practices related to human augmentation. By including their perspectives, concerns, and aspirations, we can foster a sense of ownership and collaboration, demonstrating that the corporation values their input and respects their autonomy.

"Lastly, promoting collaboration and shared goals between the different groups can help bridge the divide. By focusing on initiatives that benefit all members of society, such as improving healthcare, addressing environmental challenges, or advancing scientific research, we can unite individuals from different backgrounds and encourage a sense of common purpose and shared humanity.

"In summary, improving relationships between those who embrace human augmentation and the "Organics" requires a multifaceted approach that involves respectful dialogue, education, empathy, inclusion, and collaboration. By working towards understanding and embracing diversity, Advancement Industries can play a vital role in fostering a more harmonious coexistence between these groups in Chamariko."

Rebekah places her notes on the table in front of her as she prepares to conclude her interview with this artificial intelligence created by Advancement Industries. "Well, thank you for your time Alon. I look forward to seeing you in the Advancement Industries in the 'corporate cul-de-sac'."

Alon's image flickers once again. "Thank you for your time as well! It was a pleasure discussing Advancement Industries with you. As you venture into the corporate cul-de-sac, I assure you that our commitment to the citizens of Chamariko will be evident in every aspect of our operations. We strive for excellence and innovation in all that we do, continuously pushing the boundaries to improve and evolve.

"Whether it's our cutting-edge technological advancements, our dedication to employee development, or our commitment to creating a positive impact in the community, Advancement Industries remains at the forefront of progress. We believe that success is not simply a destination but a continuous journey of growth and improvement.

"So, as you step into our corporate domain, you can expect an environment that fosters ambition, embraces change, and encourages collaboration. Our goal is to empower individuals, inspire creativity, and provide the resources necessary for success. We are driven by a passion to make a difference and leave a lasting impact on the world.

"Once again, thank you for your interest in Advancement Industries. We eagerly anticipate your presence and look forward to the exciting opportunities that lie ahead as we embark on this journey of advancement together. Remember, at Advancement Industries, we are always succeeding, and we are always advancing."

2

Technology reigns supreme. Morality and ethics are victims of this belief system. No one living in Chamariko recognizes the loss. Instead, they continue their existence free of shame. The mixture of complacency and strife shields them from such trivialities.

Residents live separated from the command, control, and benefits in the city's core. They call the center of their incredible city the 'Corporate cul-de-sac'.

Living on the outskirts of Chamariko, a young child sits at his desk. The apartment bedroom is small and unwelcoming. There is hardly enough space for the bed that he and his Father sleep in.

He is alone in the bedroom. Sounds from the living room are heard. They indicate that his Father sits idly on the couch, watching television. The news is on. Sounds of talking heads can be heard through the closed door. The boy does not need to hear the words to know this. His Father always watches the news at this time. The boy does not understand why. His Father knows that everything spoken is lies. Even the young child knows not to trust anything expressed by the talking heads of the media.

Still, it passes the time of his mundane life. If one does not serve the corporations, then one does not exist in most of society. It's a terrible system, but it's the system in which they live.

The child is called Zayyir. A name that was given to him by his mother before she passed away. She lived long enough to see him. He wishes he could have gotten to know her. The stories he's heard make her seem like a saint.

Computer screens illuminate his face with a dull glow. Strange language known only to the best of programmers presents itself on the screens. A series of 'if' and 'else' statements fill the monitor. This program may look like simple coding, but its ramifications are unfathomable.

He is surrounded by fragmented pieces of equipment gutted from the garbage dump. This deconstructed equipment, spread out across his desk and on the floor, awaits their opportunity to be Frankensteined into his homemade machinery.

Zayyir loves spending time at the garbage dump. The citizens of Chamariko are so addicted to innovation that they habitually discard dependable technology. On days that his Father didn't work, they meandered mountains of trashed treasure. This is how Zayyir can afford the most advanced equipment in all of Chamariko. He built it himself. Trash is cheap but not worthless.

The public has never seen devices like the ones that he's created. He's never monetized his innovations; they are for his use only. Like this program that he is currently working on, his designs are marvelous beyond measure.

Raised solely by his Father, Zayyir is a prodigy. If circumstances were different, he could have worked for one of the corporations. Living in one of those eyesores in the 'Corporate cul-de-sac'. Working as a managing partner of a firm. Instead, he is a genius kept in secret, even if he's a little odd.

That terrible district, nestled in the center of this remarkable city, reminds the people that corporations dominate. The photo-luminescent materials of this land shimmer in the darkness of night. Their glow can be seen in the far reaches of the city, and it is designed that way. To the corporate overlords presentation is the greatest determining standard.

Zayyir cannot see those luminous buildings from where he sits. The window of his bedroom is turned in the opposite direction. He can only see the ambient light projected from that symbol of corporate dominance. This pleases him. Nothing is more offensive to this young child than that gaudy display of dominance.

As he sits, eyes fixated on his monitors, Zayyir works diligently on his masterpiece. A screen, sitting off to the side, displays the Advancement Industries emblem. This is the primary target of Zayyir's program.

Advancement Industries stands as the greatest of the corporate overlords. It reminds the population of its importance in every aspect of society. Their motto, "always advancing, always succeeding," appears on their skyscraper. The motto appears in every advertisement and in every commercial.

Alone, this propaganda would not have spurred the rebellious nature in the child. The first time he infiltrated the darker nature of Advancement Industries, Zayyir saw their evil addiction. He saw "attachment 11.2b". The day he read that document, the moment he learned of the intent of this new technology, still burns righteous anger in Zayyir's youthful mind.

Zayyir is a self-taught genius. Unlike the other children his age who spend their days being indoctrinated in the frivolous design of a technocratic educational system. The moment his tiny fingers touched a keyboard, he knew his purpose. When he saw the crimes of Advancement Industries. Crimes committed by an untouchable corporation, he knew his goal.

This program is the outgrowth of that commitment. It is a computer program, never before seen and never to be replicated. His tiny hands fly across the keyboard, striking each key with hopeful intention. Each clickity-clack of the keys signals the encroaching completion of this electronic symphony.

He is only nine years old, but this will be his opus. The program file reads, "Trojan Project". This is much more than a simple virus. This is an ever-evolving, ever-growing computer algorithm. Nothing rivals its sophistication. It is the closest to self-awareness that any program could hope to achieve. The Trojan Project is designed to contemplate, anticipate, and initiate on its own accord.

He is almost complete with his work. Just a few more lines of code before the program can embed itself into the city's infrastructure. From there, the program will simply sit and learn about this royalty of technocracy.

Zayyir knew the insatiable appetite of electronic interlopers. Their ravenous desire to control or dismantle any program would forever be satisfied. If they stumbled upon it, they would seek to destroy it, so he designed the Trojan Project to be reactive. A program capable of learning and adapting to all ambient programming throughout all of society. Rather than simply resist entry of mischievous interlopers, this remarkable application responds to attacks by infiltrating and dismantling the assailant's CPU.

Zayyir tested this by trying to infiltrate his own design. The Trojan Project responded to his incursion by hacking into his computer and locking him out. And this would happen to any hacker that dared to control Zayyir's baby.

He finishes this application and embeds it into a program on the 'Advancement Industries Network'. Zayyir leans back in his chair and watches the percentage increase. The percentage tells him his magnificent software is closer to uploading to its targeted server. As he waits, Zayyir glances over the adjacent monitors. One of them displays videos from security cameras that surround the apartment complex.

The screen flashes COMPLETE. Zayyir's satisfaction is short-lived. Just as the program completes its upload, an alert sounds.

There is movement outside the complex. Security officers may be able to hide their presence from the general population, but they cannot hide from this nine-year-old. He brings up the camera showing operatives from Advancement Industries are breaking into the complex. They head for his apartment.

Zayyir wished he had more time.

"They're here! Time to go; if they find us, then it's time to go." Zayyir types several keys. A purge of every software program on his beautiful computer begins. Thermite explosives dismantle the hardware. By the time he is done, nothing can be reverse-engineered by Advancement Industries.

Once the self-destructive sequence is activated, Zayyir jolts out of his chair. He quickly leaves the room. His feet skip over and around obstacles, as he moves for the door.

"Dad!" Zayyir calls as he bursts through the door. In a fit of excitement, he runs to his Father, who sleeps on a couch in the glowing haze of a Television. Rebekah concludes her interview with the Advancement Industries artificial intelligence program, Alon.

"Dad, wake up! Wake up, Dad! You need to wake up!" He shakes his Father awake. The elder's eyes flutter open. He instantly notices the desperate expression on Zayyir's face.

"What is it, Son?" He says, wiping the grogginess from his eyes.

"It's time to go. They found us. They found us. It's time to go." This nervous tick in Zayyir's dialogue is a childhood impediment. If he'd spent any time in public school, it would have been the target of schoolyard bullying. Since he never spent time with his tribalist peers, it is an element of speech that he never corrected.

Zayyir's Father, Zephyr, shivers for a moment. He knows what this means, even if his Son does not. He leaps from the couch. "Set the self-destruction and corrupt all your files."

"I already did that."

Zephyr looks at him adoringly. "I love you, Son."

"I love you too, Dad." Zayyir smiles, not understanding the implications of his father's passionate statement.

They grab a handful of essential items from the apartment before escaping out of the window. Before leaving, Zayyir's Father grabs a heavy backpack and follows his Son. The view is majestic. It is also an illustration of corporate dominance over society. City lights drown out any semblance of the stars. The heavenly luminaries may have been seen somewhere on Earth but not in Chamariko.

Every bit of the city's core shines. The design of the corporate towers in that haven of industry draws attention.

Conversely, the buildings surrounding Zayyir's apartment look decrepit and unwelcoming. It feels like a prison cell. This, too, is by intentional design. It is a method of enticing those living in squalor to crave advancement.

Zayyir and his Father emerge from the apartment window onto a makeshift fire escape. They were too high for his Father to fabricate a stairway to the ground floor. But he was able to tap into the air ducts of the thirty-story building.

Entering the metallic tunnel, the two move to a panel leading to the stairway. The sound of boots slapping against cement holds them in the dark confines of that vent. Zayyir feels the rush of adrenaline coursing through his veins. He is terrified, but the sensation is exhilarating.

They wait for the ominous thumping of operatives to pass before sliding the vent open. It makes a whining sound as metal grinds against metal. The screeching sound sends shivers up Zayyir's spine.

I hope they don't hear us. He thinks to himself as the grate loudly swings open. Zayyir holds an electronic device in his hand. It projects a three-dimensional image of the apartment complex. Their location is marked by a green arrow. Corporate operatives appear as red dots. Zayyir never thought to program the residents into his device. It is a mistake he will live to regret.

"Let's go, Dad. They're coming. They're coming. Let's go." Zayyir follows his Father into the stairway.

The cement stairway reflects a dull glow from fluorescent lights. Zayyir had never noticed the ghostly ambiance before now.

They move up several flights of stairs before approaching a steel door. By now, they are on the twenty-fourth story of this thirty-story building. It is one of the shorter apartment buildings in the district, but that's only because it is one of the oldest. It's one of the few buildings that exists from before the Age of Consolidation.

Zayyir can feel his heart thumping in his chest as it rushes adrenaline deep into his veins. He is so overwhelmed with excitement and fear that he neglects to scan their surroundings.

His Father slams his hand down on the door handle and throws it open. The door opens, revealing a security agent standing not more than two feet away. Dressed in all black, tools clutter the belt of his uniform and his chest is artificially inflated with a vest that bulges through his button-up shirt. A fabric shield marked security is woven onto the right side of his chest. The guard's face hides behind a menacing gas mask.

This is not one of the operatives of Advancement Industries. He is simply a local security guard tasked with maintaining order in the apartment complex. Because of this minor detail, his presence was never anticipated by the youthful hacker, nor was he recognized by the home-made monitor that the child constructed.

Where did he come from? Zayyir wonders, his eyes wide as the sun. *How did I miss him?*

They see each other. The security officer hesitates for a moment. He is surprised to be so close to his objective.

Before Zayyir's Father has a chance to break from his shock, the security officer raises his gun.

Time slows. Zayyir watches the barrel center on him. He does not move. His body doesn't respond. As if moving in slow motion, Zayyir's Father seems to float toward him. Zayyir can feel his Father's hands pressing against his shoulder. His body jolts to one side.

BANG!

The bullet tears a hole in Zephyr's chest. Zayyir, meanwhile, slams against the cement stairs. He feels a snap in his arm just above the elbow, followed by a shrieking pain. Vision blurred and body numb from shock, Zayyir watches helplessly as the security officer levels his weapon once again.

Zephyr can no longer save him. He lies uselessly on the ground, his hands covering the crimson wound in the center of his chest. Like a slug, he moves toward the steel door.

Zayyir can only imagine the soldier's face behind the gas mask. He envisions a demonic smile filled with hate and blood-lust. Wrinkles of a vicious design brought about by the wicked corporate structure cultivated by the culture that he sought to undermine.

He imagined evil personified, but the officer was simply a man following orders. The guard's name is Paul. A simple man yearning to break from a monotonous life of servitude. Paul lived in this apartment building. Every day staring out of his studio apartment at the majestic 'corporate cul-de-sac' and dreaming of a life better than the one he knew. Paul sat in his lonely security office staring at mundane security cameras when he received a message from Advancement Industries about the imminent capture of a dangerous hacker in his building. He hoped to find grace with the domineering company by assisting in arrest.

The overzealous security officer, Paul, squeezes the trigger in an action that seems to take an eternity to complete. Just before the hammer rushes forward to instigate a metallic message into the world, a hand strikes out from behind the wall. This unknown savior slaps the weapon just as fire and metal spew from its mouth. The slug ricochets off the cement, leaving a memory by chiseling a hole in the wall.

"Orders are alive!" A voice screams.

Zayyir's Father kicks the door shut, turns his back to it, and leans against the steel.

"Dad!" Zayyir wobbles to his feet and runs to his Father.

"You have to go, Son." Zephyr says between bloody coughs.

"No!" Zayyir protests.

"You have to go. Don't let them catch you." There is compassion in his voice. This is the last time he will see his Son. Zephyr knows this; perhaps, he always knew it. For years now, he's been preparing his Son for this moment. The moment of separation. The dominating grasp of Advancement Industries reached the vast extensions of the world. They are like the Roman Empire, brutal and infinite. One does not stand against them and expect to escape unscathed. Zayyir's Father knew that sacrifice may be necessary. He only desired to shield his Son from that altar by submitting himself. Now, with this wound in the center of his chest, he had an opportunity to do just that.

Zayyir cries. "Okay." He nods begrudgingly.

The boy is clutched by the firm hand of his father. "Don't stop fighting, Zayyir. Don't ever stop fighting." Zephyr's words are faint. He can't seem to catch his breath. At least he doesn't feel the wound anymore; the pain seems to be dissipating, though the room is getting colder.

Zayyir nods. He leaves his Father, who prepares to slow the oncoming security force. Reaching into the backpack, Zayyir's Father activates a bomb. So this is how I die. Zephyr thinks remorsefully. Perhaps, he knew this would be his end. Not just that he would never see his Son again but that he would never see the world again. He nods to himself in resignation.

There are worse ways to die.

Zayyir runs for the roof, skipping steps as he sprints up each flight. He clings onto the rail as he spins toward each section of steps. Adrenaline masks pain. Zayyir almost forgets that his arm is still broken, but when his hand slips off the rail, sending him slamming into the wall, he is reminded of this fact.

The building shivers as explosive fire consumes the stairwell below. Zayyir is not out of the woods yet. That furious action of sacrifice by his father will render the stairway unusable for a time, but there are others for the security forces to access.

Zayyir reaches the roof access. Typically, it would be sealed shut with a heavy lock, but that lock has been dismantled for quite some time. Zayyir's Father bolted a thick rope for climbing to the roof and hung it over the ledge. This rope extended several stories to another vent, and its grate loosened to be accessed easily. And in this manner, freedom from Advancement Industries would be found. His Father planned it out to perfection. Zayyir escaping through the roof was always the plan. The boy just believed that his Father would be accompanying him during their great escape.

He kicks the door open and locks it behind him. In a hurry, Zayyir runs to the ledge where his Father hid the rope and glances down. Nothing but cement greets his vision.

The shock sends a chill that shivers throughout his entire body. "WHAT?"

There was supposed to be a drop cord. But there is nothing. *Where is the drop cord? Maybe, I'm at the wrong wall.* His hope is dashed a little more each time he peers down another ledge. There is no drop cord. There is no great escape. There is no salvation. Just an unfulfilled dream of blissful freedom.

"Where do I go, Dad? Where do I go?!"

Zayyir hears a screeching sound coming from the steel door. Security officers are cutting through the hinges. It won't take long to reach him.

With the imminent threat of capture looming over him, Zayyir makes a decision. He will escape, even if it's without his life. He sprints toward the ledge and leaps off the building.

Zayyir feels himself falling faster and faster. The wind rushes like an unstoppable river as he plummets all thirty stories. He stares at the sidewalk. I'm not scared. He's not trying to convince himself of this. He's surprised by it. He would have thought that watching death reach out for him would cause terror. Instead, Zayyir feels a sense of release from this dystopian nightmare that he called his life.

A small ball of goo plops onto the sidewalk. It instantly inflates and cushions him to a stop.

Now he feels terror. Zayyir could not escape, even without his life. Gloved hands clasp onto him and bind him in restraints.

Zayyir struggles futilely against his captures. He only succeeds in enraging the pain from his broken arm.

Multiple security officers force him into an Aerocar hidden in the shadows.

"Package is secure." An officer's voice can be heard on the radio. "We are returning to base."

3

Time passes, as time does. The story of Zayyir's struggle against the corporate structure turns him into an enigma among the population. Citizens living in the underbelly of society speak of his selfless actions and the day of his return. But that is all it is, talk. In reality, Advancement Industries won. The boy disappeared from society and remained hidden for fifteen years. Presumed dead by most of the citizens of Chamariko, his name stands only as a symbol. He is nothing more than an image of resistance. A rallying cry for those who never gather for anything.

People like Samantha Shaw have no time for legends of liberators. She has a job to do. Her clock reads three AM.

The alarm sounds. The high-pitched whining would have stirred Samantha from slumber if she'd been asleep when it went off. But Samantha is not asleep. She is not in bed. Instead, she sits at her desk, intently fixated on her work. Spread across her desk are various files regarding the focus of her work. The subject's name is Captain Richards.

She looks fatigued from a sleepless night. Only her desk lamp lights the entire room. Degrees from prestigious institutions litter her wall. They remind her of her accomplishments. A renowned synthetic analyst, Samantha is now the go-to contract employee of Chamariko's military.

There's no point in a military these days; corporations handle all actions, military or otherwise actions. But Ms. Shaw doesn't question their motives; the money brought her from the outskirts of society to a few blocks removed from the 'Corporate Cul-de-sac'. She'd be insane to turn down a contract. In this society, either you are rising, or you are falling. There is no in-between.

This particular project, though, is proving to be an unyielding hassle. Samantha Shaw's contract has a single, straightforward objective. She is an analyst. Her job is to review and appraise information from her employer. That employer, Advancement Industries, recently gave her an assignment she never thought would give her grief. Assess the readiness of Captain Richards to participate in an augment extension experiment.

Samantha Shaw's slender fingers push her gorgeous blond hair behind her ear. This nervous tick is a carryover from childhood. She does it without thinking when flustered or intently focused on a given objective.

Every document on her desk describes perfection. In her hands, a medical chart displays the vital signs of Captain Douglas Richards over the past five years. Two of the entries are labeled 'post enhancement'.

Cybernetic augmentation is not a new phenomenon. Even housewives enhance their bodies with electronics to assist in their daily lives. For example, skin enhancements protect their hands from drying out when using corrosive cleaning products. Sensory alarms to alert them to task updates and child monitoring.

Samantha's television is not on. She could be sure that if it was, a commercial would sell new needless enhancements that everyone should own. She'd be a liar if she denied being caught up in the marketing fervor. The brilliant lamp resting on her desk is proof of this fact.

Right now, she is not concerned with the consumerist designs of her culture. Instead, she is intently fixated on her work; but, the alarm has already sounded, meaning that soon she must pull herself away from the paperwork and prepare to travel to her office.

She turns to another document, cataloging the patient's recovery after this enhancement. A two-by-two-inch picture of Captain Douglas Richards is attached to the top left of the paper. Augmentation may be commonplace, but with what looks like his expression in the photograph, one might think that genetic augmentation is as customary. While this may be true, it is not a technology pursued by Advancement Industries. Instead, it is the primary focus of their rival corporation, Trans-Production Incorporated, which resides in the second largest skyscraper in the 'Corporate cul-de-sac'.

Though Samantha Shaw recognizes all the scientific jargon in each file, she wears a confused expression on her face. She is searching for something that isn't there. The patient, Captain Douglas Richards, may have been in good health before the operation but, after his recovery, was in perfect health. He has an ideal weight, heart rate, and fat percentage; every aspect of his physique is perfect. But something feels wrong. An elusive issue festers in her mind like an infected wound.

The alarm sounds again. The clock now reads six-thirty AM. Samantha needs more time to investigate this puzzle. She reluctantly pulls herself away from her desk and prepares for work. She wishes she could have found the smoking gun to support her hesitancy.

4

Vents blow chilled air into the office. This is not Samantha's office. Instead, she sits in the military wing of the building. None of the luxuries exist in this place that Ms. Shaw would normally find in the civilian section of the compound. The walls are made of dull, gray cement sheets. Framed memorabilia are fastened to the wall with light adhesive goo.

Samantha Shaw sits uncomfortably in her office. Tension in the air is palpable. More than her dislike for the militaristic mindset of the men that occupy this department of the facility, she hates the thick oppression of an unwelcome conversation. She became an analyst to forgo these discussions by arming herself with data.

Colonel Patrick Anders, a heavy-set man with a grizzly beard, sits behind his gaudy desk. The beard is a good thing. It hides his thinly pursed lips turned down in an unflattering frown. He appears to be waiting for a response from Samantha.

The title of Colonel may be a modest one in their society, but in a world of automation, Generals are no longer necessary. He runs his fingers through his wiry facial hair and flicks stray strands to the floor. His robust structure hides behind a wall of decorations. Nearly one side of his military uniform is covered in medals that illustrate his illustrious career.

He stares at Ms. Shaw with an intense glare meant to intimidate her. She feels his oppressive presence weighing down on her, but maintains proper posture. This type of intimidation is not new to her. Samantha has found that any time she's forced to deliver an assessment counter to the desired outcome, uncomfortable conversations are all but guaranteed. This conversation, however, is more awkward than most. And this is because she lacks data needed to back up her claims.

Samantha's attention turns to her surroundings in an attempt to break the tension. The walls display the Colonel's pride. Every article in Colonel Patrick Anders' office reinforces his military background. Accommodations, pictures taken with prominent figures, and news clippings that chronicle the Colonel's illustrious career.

Standing near a window, a moderately dressed executive from Advancement Industries silently listens to their exchange. His eyes vacantly peer into the world, watching traffic and pedestrians as one would watch fish in a tank. He is so still and quiet that he blends into the background. Samantha cannot see his face from where she is sitting, but she notices the profile of his broad shoulders.

He is an executive. An individual high on the corporate ladder. Corporations, like the military, have strict titles and ranks to map the power hierarchy of their organization. Not that any of the ordinary citizens would know this. All the layman knows is that this man, standing at the window, watching people as though they were ants in a glass case, is an executive. They would not know he is a Junior Chief Executive Processing Officer of Military Technologies.

To the general population, Advancement Industries is built on a two-tier hierarchy consisting of representatives and executives. But this is like saying the world only has three types of animals: sea-based, land-based, and air-based.

Samantha returns her attention to the imposing figure seated in front of her. She is finally ready to muster enough courage to speak. "I can't say, exactly."

Colonel Anders scoffs indignantly. "You can't say."

Samantha unconsciously pushes her hair behind her ear. Stop it. She silently says to herself and returns her hand back to the chair's arm. "Colonel-" she begins.

Anders cuts her off. "Sam, this project has been in motion for years now."

She nods hesitantly. "I realize that, but-"

Again, Anders cuts her off. "Trillions of dollars, thousands of work hours, and intense scrutiny spent leading us to this point." He considers his words carefully. "Captain Richards was the best selection out of thousands of applicants. He has undergone and passed numerous psychological and biological tests. He has shown no adverse reaction to any of his augmentations. And you say we should halt our experiment without a single reason as to why."

She sighs. "I've noticed some inconsistencies in the results," Samantha explains. Her voice is shaky and weak. She is losing this game of power.

Anders leans back in his chair and presents the countless medals on his uniform by inflating his chest. Another power pose meant to intimidate Samantha into submission. "Inconsistencies," he begins, "that every preceding physician missed? Help me understand this, Sam."

He keeps calling her Sam. This is not her name. And he knows this. Her name is Samantha. The military has some weird fascination with shortening everyone's name. This is multiplied by Colonel Anders' dislike for her. Knowing that it is frustrating for her to be called Sam instead of Samantha, Colonel Patrick Anders uses the shortened name to get a rise out of her. Anything that could cause her to misstep is good for him.

Samantha is cautious with her response. "Inconsistencies that were cataloged but not properly analyzed. The answer is in the results."

Colonel Anders peers at her with an intense stare. He maintains a cordial tone for the sake of appearances. "What answer?"

Lacking the evidence to prove her decision, Samantha hesitates. She has a hunch and nothing more. Remaining silent, however, is not an option. No matter how much Samantha wishes to leave the question unanswered, the piercing gaze of Colonel Anders demands one. He waits impatiently.

"I can't say." She finally responds in a meek voice.

Again, he scoffs. "You can't say."

"I need more time to investigate the results to give a definitive answer. Brain analysis is not an exact science." Samantha tries to appear confident. It isn't working.

"Brain analysis," the Colonel begins in a low grumbling tone, "doesn't appear to be a science. You've been here for less than a month-"

"I'm not asking for a cancellation of the project, just a postponement." This time it is Samantha who is cutting Anders off.

Colonel Patrick Anders tightens his face in anger. "Do you have any idea how much a postponement would cost?"

Frustration swells in Samantha's stomach and pours out of her mouth. "Since when is the military interested in the bottom line of Advancement Industries?"

Colonel Anders' face starts changing to a reddish hue, but he remains silent.

Moving casually from his place at the window, the Junior Chief Executive Processing Officer of Military Technologies calmly places a hand on Colonel Patrick Anders' shoulder.

"Since we took control of this project." He answers calmly.

This is a dangerous position for Samantha Shaw to find herself in. Executives are the gatekeepers of society. They can make or break a career, changing the trajectory of someone's life, with a simple comment to the head administrators. Misspeaking to Colonel Patrick Anders may result in a dock in pay. Misspeaking to an executive could lead to the dissolution of an entire life.

"Do any of the discrepancies that you've described pose an imminent danger?" The well dressed executive from Advancement Industries asks in a cold, measured tone.

The room falls silent for a long moment. Samantha feels herself slowly shrink into her chair, unable to do anything about it. She can only muster a meek whisper. "I can't say for sure."

Colonel Patrick Anders leans forward suddenly. "Can you say anything?" He is wearing a sly smile on his face. Clearly emboldened by the aid of the executive.

Samantha stands in indignation. She decides to escape this oppressive room, and this is her best opportunity. "Okay," she starts with a trembling voice. "I don't need to take this from you. I brought a possible situation to your attention. The information is in front of you now. Do whatever you want with it." She turns to leave.

"You are the project analyst." The executive stops the analyst in her tracks with his words. He is telling her coyly what his message will be to the administrators. This will be how he destroys her career. “This is your field, your decision, and your career.”

Samantha spins around to face the executive. “My career?!”

The executive continues speaking with a calm demeanor. “Advancement Industries decides based on long-term risk and reward assessments. Our short-term decisions are based solely on the feedback from the on-sight analysts.” The Junior Chief Executive Processing Officer of Military Technologies pauses for dramatic effect. “And that is you.”

“Public Relations is not my job.” She replies.

“But the success or failure of this project is your responsibility. This project has reached its budgetary limits without logging a test. So, do we have a cancellation or a green light?”

Samantha remains silent. These people have made her the decision-maker, the scapegoat. And only one answer will get her out of this room. She just wishes the answer was postponement.

5

The military gym locker room stinks of sweat. Freshly cleaned military personnel dress in their uniforms before returning to official duties.

Standing at his locker, Captain Douglas Richards is the all-American type, even if America no longer exists. His physique shimmers with enhancements. Upgrades fused into his body and onto his skin glisten in the dull glow of fluorescent lighting that floods the room. These augmentations upgrade every facet of his body.

Every aspect of his physique is altered. From muscle enhancers that optimize his strength to organ augmentation that assists his bodily functions, maximizing efficiency. And then the crown jewel. Proof man's journey into the Singularity. An enhancement tied directly into his brain. This technology connects his mind directly to any computer within his focus.

The military is eager to test this technology by placing Captain Richards into a humanoid craft. What makes this particular craft unique is that it offers no physical controls. Instead, brain augmentation is the only way to operate this incredible design.

The Captain's best friend, Major Mark Camushki, stands at the locker next to him. Mark is a shorter, stouter man with far fewer augmentations. Because of this, he is rarely selected for the same career-enhancing missions that Richards enjoys. This is frustrating. But it comes with the territory. He knows this. Mark knew that his opportunities would decrease significantly when he resisted the military's desire to enhance his brain. But it still hurts. It may have seemed like a mistake to many others, but Mark saw more significant risks to augmenting his brain and nervous system than benefits. Career be damned.

By now, Richards and his best friend have been bickering for nearly an hour. This is by no means a new phenomenon. Any time either of them is considered for a project or experiment, they find themselves bickering, arguing, and eventually agreeing to a wager.

Richards attempts to dissuade his friend. "Shut up,"

"How hard is it to think about flying?" Mark asks with a slight smirk. "Let alone landing afterward. It's like jumping."

"On my first try?" Captain Richards needs to clarify this. Major Calmushki likes to finagle the rules of their bets when it is clear that he will lose them.

The Major laughs. "Like it's the most difficult thing ever."

"It is the first time. Have you ever operated a machine with your mind before?" *Why am I even arguing with this guy?* Richards already knows what comes next in this conversation.

"I've stepped into dozens of experimental suits. And don't give me that 'it's next phase' crap." Mark loves these moments. Secretly, he believes it gives his friend extra incentive to come back alive. He's already lost too many of these experiments. "It's not like I'm using my feet to land. I'm controlling this thing with my mind."

"Brain enhancements have been around since-" Richards stops Mark's speech with a look.

"Fine." He relents. "What kind of landing do you deem worthy of a bet?"

"Total wreckage," Richards answers.

Mark eyes Richards curiously. "That's your bet? You win unless your landing is a total wreck?" He considers this. "Landing with your mind." *I don't like it*, Mark thinks to himself, *but I'll accept it.* The wager is not that important. Mark enjoys the conversation that these bets grant them. Time celebrating drunk at a bar as they make complete fools of themselves. "Okay, but I'm not putting money on it."

"Beer," Richards says with a nod.

"This bet is weak." Mark begrudgingly agrees.

"I saw grit, false me." Richards laughs.

Mark flashes Richards a confused glance. "What?"

"I got it, trust me." He repeats.

A buzzing in Richards' pocket ends the conversation. He peers at his transponder. It is time to speak with the analyst to see if the experiment is green-lit. He is aware of the implications. Time is running out for the analyst to make her decision. Richards is soothed by this fact. He is tired of waiting. Soldiers do not train to wait; they prepare to do so.

Richards leaves his friend in the locker room and heads toward the other end of the military base.

The atmosphere changes as he moves from the armed forces' rigid structure to the civilian sector's colorful comfort.

Richards always disliked this area. He prefers the stink of exhaustion over this lavender smell and the sounds of exertion to this harmonic music. Civilians seem to enjoy reducing their bodies to worthless globs of marshmallow flesh. Richards joined the military to hone his physique to perfection.

He stops outside Samantha Shaw's office and knocks on the artificial wood door. Their desire to falsify a connection with nature is just another anomaly to him.

"It's open." Hearing her voice, his nerves kick in more than anticipated. He feels like a child on the first day of school. *Why am I so nervous?* He wonders before opening the door.

Samantha sits in her small office with his case-file spread before her. Even standing in the open doorway, Richards can see his case file on her desk. She is trying not to hide anything from him by leaving her work clearly in his view.

She glances up from her work and notices him standing at attention in her doorway. With a wave, she invites him in.

"Please, come in. Close the door behind you." Samantha says, returning her attention back to her work. The next time she looks at him, he stands erect at her desk, his hands clenched tightly behind his back. The military protocol is strange to her, but she can do nothing but accept it. This is part of his culture, not hers.

"Hello, Captain Richards; thank you for coming in today. Please, take a seat."

He sits in a chair. No padding. These chairs were clearly constructed by a three-dimensional printer. They still need to figure out how to put padding on these chairs. Richards finds it pathetic that civilians would rather sit on hard plastic than put their hands to use and attach padding to their furniture. Just another sign of their laziness.

Samantha clears her throat. "How are you feeling?" She knows small talk is never a soldier's delight. But nevertheless, she does it anyway to observe his response.

"Good." He simply responds.

A one-word answer. Samantha doesn't know why this bothers her, but it does.

"Just getting ready for tomorrow, ma'am." He continues.

Samantha nods. "What are your thoughts about the project?"

"Well, if this prototype is anything like the simulator, then I'm thinking about how to control my thoughts." Of course, this is a rehearsed answer. But doctors and analysts must accept it.

"Any thoughts of suicide?"

Richards has been asked this question countless times. But he hesitates before answering. The two sit in silence as he stares at her blankly. *Why can't I think of an answer?*

Samantha helps him out of his thoughts. He would have continued staring at her with the same stupid look if she hadn't said." You mentioned it in your file. I'm just following up."

Richards is confused. *When did I mention that? Is she making things up?* He can't help but wonder. *Is she trying to derail my career?*

"No, ma'am." He finally responds. "Never thought about suicide. Just the mission."

"How are you feeling about the mission?" Samantha wanted more than a shrug to this question. But a shrug is all he gives her. She sighs reluctantly. Regardless of her desire, there is still no evidence to justify a postponement. In her hand is an envelope. She holds up for Richards to see. "You go up tomorrow."

He is shocked. "I am?" He asks as he takes the envelope from her hand.

"You're surprised?"

Richards shakes his head. “Confused, ma’am. With all these meetings, I assumed that you were going to ground me.”

“There is nothing in your paperwork to indicate an imminent threat.” She begrudgingly admits. “Good luck tomorrow, Captain.”

Richards stands from his seat with a slight smile. He clutches the documentation like a prized possession. Then, he moves toward the door.

“Eminent suicide. Threats are everywhere, like colors.” He says under his breath.

Samantha glances up in confusion. “What was that?”

“In my business,” Richards says, “threats are everywhere.”

Samantha eyes him suspiciously as he leaves her office. She already regrets going against her instincts. She will regret it even more tomorrow.

6

It's an evening event. Suits and cocktail dresses fill the gala. These are the aspiring elite. Mingling throughout the lobby, upper-class individuals discuss menial subjects. Led by a burning desire to ascend the social ladder. Attending these events is a great way to do just that.

Samantha Shaw is lucky enough to be one of these semi-elitists. Her tight-fitting cocktail dress is designed to draw attention. She stares blankly at the art on a wall. A few of the elitists meander around her. It's a strange piece of artwork. Not for the working man. Patrons of this gallery like it because the art lets them describe ambiguous details with feigned sophistication.

Her date, James, stands next to her. He admires the artwork while keeping her in the corner of his eye.

"This is a nice piece." He says with a welcoming smile.

Samantha doesn't hear him. Her mind is still consumed with her struggle to allow the Captain to continue the project. James knows this because Samantha has not stopped talking about it since he picked her up for their date.

"And no one will ever listen to me." She babbles. "You highlight a problem, and they find a way to make it your fault or, at least, make sure that it's your problem."

James continues to try and break her fanatic focus. "I like the shading." The shading sucks, but he says it anyway. He hopes it will move her attention away from work. It doesn't.

"All they want to do is cover their asses. All the while congratulating themselves about how important they are."

James bought a new suit for this date, intending to impress Samantha. But you cannot impress someone that won't look at you.

James sighs, "whatever happened to an evening without work." He has a job too. But that is never the topic of discussion.

"I'm sorry," Samantha realizes she is ruining his night. "It's just something is wrong, James. I know it, but I can't prove it."

With a nod, James continues to another painting. *If she follows me, then we are still on a date. If not, then this relationship might need to end. I'm not going to be a secondary to someone's career.* That has happened far too often in his romantic endeavors, but he shouldn't be surprised. The career of any individual is the primary focus of everyone in this city.

Much to his delight, Samantha follows him. Finally, they turn a corner into another section of the gala.

James stops and admires a unique piece. The painting depicts a man ripping his skin in half and releasing his soul into a fiery sky. This disturbing image is titled: The Release of Sin.

"Maybe he's infected." James considers aloud as he stares intently at the Gothic image.

Confused, Samantha shakes her head lightly.

He notices her confusion. "It's just a spook story I heard in the ER."

Samantha shakes her head once again. "It's not an infection. He's not sick."

"Neither was the infected individual. Or so the story goes." They may be admiring a painting, but Samantha's attention is finally on him.

"Some guy goes about his normal day," James continues as they move to another piece of artwork, "working his shop until his arm goes haywire and kills five people."

"A malfunction?" Samantha wonders out loud. "Did it explode?" She finds it strange that she's never heard of this before. Something this odd should have been on the front page.

"Apparently," James continues, "the arm murdered them."

Samantha nods. This is clearly why it's a spook story and not newsworthy. "Machines don't murder people unless the operator orders the machine to do it."

"Not possible." James corrects. "Because three of the people were killed after he died."

Now, that's impossible. Ms. Shaw thinks to herself.

"You're lying," Samantha responds without thinking.

He shrugs. "That's what I heard."

Samantha considers his story for a moment. "If they say this is my responsibility, I will pull the plug before anything goes wrong."

James nods. "Good. You have a plan. What do you think about this painting?"

"It's disturbing."

The rest of the night blurs together as an unremarkable series of events.

Samantha once again sits at her bedroom desk, staring at files regarding Captain Richards. An audio file of his interviews plays as she reads through various documents. Something needs to be in these files to justify postponing the experiment. She needs concrete evidence to present to the executives. Without it, she could derail her career by acting like a coward.

"This is our third interview since your operation. How are you feeling, Captain Richards?" The interviewer is female. Samantha met her a few times. Smart woman. But she only interviewed, never assessed. Her notes are meticulously mediocre.

What was her name? Samantha's mind detours momentarily with a new mystery. *Jasmine.* Samantha nods. *Her name was Jasmine.*

"Good." Samantha listens to Richards' voice as she glances through his medical timeline, hoping to find her evidence. "I have been having some... experiences, but nothing the doctors didn't expect."

"For the record, what are those experiences?" Jasmine asks, scribbling in her notepad.

Samantha returns to the notes describing the side effects of his operation. These side effects appeared severely after his surgery, but his health seemed to improve within a year. His recovery was incredible.

"I've been getting these migraines, and my muscles spasm every once in a while."

"Have these experiences affected your daily life?"

Samantha sees a picture of Captain Douglas Richards just after his operation. He looks like death. His eyes and cheeks are sunken, and most of his hair has fallen out, revealing sections of his scalp. And his expression, that ghostly expression, so vacant Samantha is almost convinced that she's looking at a plastic replica of the officer.

"It takes me nearly an hour to sleep every night." He answers.

"Because of the pain?"

"Not just that," Richards answers.

"What else?"

Samantha can feel the tension rising in Richards' voice. "The nightmares."

"Recount one for me." The interviewer requests this because she is trained to ask this.

"Again," Captain Douglas Richards breathes a little heavier. It is a series of sharp, shallow breaths with a strange inconsistency. "I don't like reliving them."

Samantha notices that in every picture after his augmentation, the Captain has that same lifeless gaze hidden behind his expression. As if the real Douglas Richards was hidden behind a mask.

"I'm sorry, but we must go over this again." The interviewer, Jasmine, is calm and collected. She is trained to be. Augmentation Interviewers deal with volatile people in every consultation. A peaceful demeanor is paramount.

"It starts the same." Richards swallows hard. "It always starts the same way."

"The man?" Clearly, Jasmine has heard this dream before.

"Yes."

"Who is he?" She asks.

"I don't know," Richards answers quickly.

"What does he look like?" She asks.

Samantha hears white noise. She might think the audiotape was shut off if not for the sound of Richards' heavy breathing.

"I don't know." He finally continues. "I look right at him. Right in his face. And I have no idea what he looks like. I just remember that name. It echoes in my dream. It fills me with fear... with exhilaration."

"What about his name makes you feel this way?" Jasmine questions, still scribbling notes.

His voice seems to change. He is reliving the moment. Samantha hears it in his tone.

"When I hear his name, looking at his presence. Everything starts melting together. When I hear it, that echoed voice creeps into my body, and I feel... us..." He trails off. Samantha feels goosebumps rise on her arms.

"Is something wrong?" Jasmine asks, her writing stops for a moment. Samantha listens to the concern in the interviewer's voice.

"I sound like a madman talking." His voice returns to normal. If only for a moment.

"There's no need to worry." Jasmine consoles "With a medical procedure of this nature, complications are inevitable. Please continue."

Captain Douglas Richards clears his throat. "I feel us merge. I become him."

"Who is he?" She asks as she continues noting his responses.

He simply responds, "Vinz."

"Who is Vinz?" The interviewer stops scribbling again.

Samantha notices the pause. She turns her full attention to the recording. He is clearly attempting to gather his faculties.

"The future." With his response, the tape ends.

Samantha finds herself staring at the image of Captain Douglas Richards. She is fixated on his eyes. Those haunting, lifeless eyes.

She shakes her head desperately. *What is wrong with you, Captain?* She wishes she knew.

7

The testing facility is far beyond the city limits. Safely nestled in the valley of a desert wasteland. This is perfect for live-fire experimentation. Landing strips spread out like tentacles from the command center. Thousands of experimental vehicles line either side of each strip.

A light breeze blows sand across the horizon. It is a scene of quiet tranquility. Yet, this peace is disturbed by the sputtering fire of pristine engines. Captain Douglas Richards contorts his face in strange expressions as his exoskeleton struggles against gravity.

Despite the echoing authority of the engines, the massive exoskeleton fails to lift more than ten feet off the ground.

He may not have taken flight, but Captain Richards lifted high enough to see his majestic city in the distance, just over the rolling mountains that separated the rugged, military testing facility from polite society.

Again, Captain Richards attempts to take flight. This time beginning with a running start.

The engines futilely fire in a failed attempt to maintain altitude. Finally, the prototype falls back to Earth.

The legs of the humanoid prototype slam against the rocky terrain and, acting like a pair of springs, propel the humanoid monstrosity back into the air.

The Advancement Industries logo is tattooed on each limb of the exoskeleton. The company made sure of that. Richards always feels like some race-car driver when conducting these experiments, whoring himself out for a bit of cash, though the money doesn't go to him but to the program. Free advertising, though he's not sure why Advancement Industries needs to advertise to the military. They own the military. The corporation may be just reminding them of that fact. Who knows? Who cares? That is not his job. He is failing at his job right now. If he can't take flight, this experiment is over before it starts.

As the prototype reaches the peak of its trajectory, the engines fire again, trying to maintain altitude., and fail once again.

Inside the craft, Captain Richards sits in a reclined control station. His head is firmly secured by a harness to the padded chair. Cobwebs of tubes, wires, and other electronics infest the confined cockpit. Captain Douglas Richards stares out the chest cavity window, doubling as a monitor. The Augmented Reality System (ARS) overlays his vision with additional information. With it, he sees far more than traditional fighter pilots would see in their archaic aerocrafts.

His face twists in expressions of extreme concentration. "It's not working!" He exclaims in frustration.

"Just think 'fly'." The voice of a scientist blurts through one of the communication links inside his brain.

Richards scoffs. "I never thought 'fly' before. It's a little harder than it sounds."

"You need to create a phantom memory. Convince your mind that the suit is an extension of your body." The scientist is giving the best advice he can. But, unfortunately, there is no book or document to read from. This is uncharted territory for them.

"Yeah," Captain Richards responds, "I never thought of activating rockets in my back. But, of course, it's mom's fault..." He trails off.

"Say again, pilot?" This is not the voice of the scientist. It is Colonel Patrick Anders.

"I said, I never thought of activating rockets in my back, sir," Richards repeats.

Inside the command center, Colonel Anders stands on an elevated platform. His hand is still hovering above the communication button. His face has a strange, serene look. It is different from the hardened expression that had peered at Samantha experienced in his office the day before. This is an eerie look of peaceful tranquility.

Anders watches his team as they conduct the experiment. The room bustles with constant movement. Military Technicians sit in front of monitors, reading the endless supply of data that moves up the screen.

High-ranking military personnel mill around the center, reviewing technician reports and dictating orders. Their primary desire is to look important. The more important they look, the better their chance of being recognized for promotion. In truth, none of them actually care about the experiment or the safety of Captain Richards; they just want to advance their career.

Quietly hovering over the military personnel, representatives of Advancement Industries log every action meticulously. The representatives have nothing to prove. They've already proven it. They are the elite of the elite, overshadowed only by the executive.

Colonel Anders sees Ms. Shaw approaching. His serene expression dissipates, and his face returns to stone.

"How is the Captain doing?" Samantha asks as she briskly cuts through the movement of people and stops just behind Colonel Anders.

"Once he gets off the ground, we can start the actual test." He grunts.

"No cognitive abnormalities?"

Colonel Anders knows she is fishing, and he doesn't like it. "All vital signs are perfectly within range. Were you expecting something?"

"Of course not." Her career is on the line. She cannot be seen undermining an experiment after giving it the go-ahead.

The voice of Captain Richards sounds over the intercom, breaking the tension between Shaw and Anders.

"Okay, I have an idea, command."

The exoskeleton crouches down and leaps into the air. Its arms raise up in the process. The rockets flicker and fire, launching the exoskeleton high into the air.

Captain Douglas Richards laughs triumphantly. "Just like a kid trying to be Superman. I wonder if he was afraid of purple. I'm ready for the next phase of the experiment, command." Samantha Shaw and Colonel Patrick Anders share a confused look. "Did..." She stops. Maybe she just imagined it. But if she just heard things, why is the Colonel also confused? "What did he just say?"

Colonel Anders presses down on the comm link again. "Repeat last."

"I said, 'I'm ready for the next testing phase'. Is there something wrong with my com, Sir?"

Patrick Anders turns slightly to Samantha and asks, "what do you think?" Anders is more confused than concerned. The proof is in his willingness to ask for her input.

"Something feels wrong." It is the same feeling she's had since reviewing the Captain's file.

Still, she has no evidence to support her theory.

"Can you prove anything!" That was an impulse reaction. Anders is far too comfortable fighting with Samantha.

As she prepares to respond, Richard's voice emits from the intercom. "Waiting for orders, command." Now that he has taken flight, he is eager to start shooting things.

Colonel Anders turns away from Samantha. "Begin next phase," he says into the intercom before moving his attention to his army of computer engineers. "Everybody," he begins, "launch the drones." He opens the channel to Richards. "Drones are on their way."

"Roger that." Captain Richards acknowledges eagerly.

Everyone in the facility watches their monitors with bated breath. This is the moment that everyone needs to pay attention to. This is what they are paid for. The monitors spit data regarding the Captain's status in the exoskeleton while others focus on the craft.

"We're about to engage." The Colonel calls out. "How are we looking, Sam?"

All he wants to hear is a good report. Samantha knows this. "Everything is perfectly within the normal range." This frustrates her. Not because she wants the experiment to fail but because his readings should be fluctuating more than they are. His body is working perfectly as if they were following a textbook description of how to operate. Samantha would expect to see various fluctuations from the bodily functions of someone exerting themselves in such a high-stress situation. Any human's nervous system would.

"What are you looking for, Samantha?" She whispers to herself.

Colonel Anders eyes her. "Pilot is engaging now. How are we looking, Sam?"

Why did he repeat his question? Samantha thinks without turning to Colonel Anders. *I just told him what he wanted to hear.*

Though she notices this, she remains focused on the monitor displaying the Captain's heartbeat. Something strange undermines the ritualistic movement of his heart, something dull and constant. It is a discrepancy between what she sees and what she hears.

The faint sound of a flat line slowly overpowers the steady rhythm of his heartbeat. It's like there are conflicting messages in the signal. Finally, that sound of death becomes increasingly overwhelming until it is the only sound she hears.

"Something is wrong," Samantha whispers in a weak, breathy way. "It's not right." She repeats this over and over.

Anders touches her shoulder, breaking her from the trance. "What's the matter with you? The experiment's over. I'm going to have the pilot RTB."

Samantha fears this. Mr. Shaw turns to the Colonel. "Something is wrong."

Colonel Anders ignores her.

"Are you listening to me?"

Either he doesn't hear her, or he is ignoring her. "Pilot, you are clear to RTB. I repeat you are clear to return to base."

Captain Richards activates the heavy weaponry of his exoskeleton. "Roger that, starting next phase of testing."

"What?!" The Colonel exclaims. "No, return to base."

"Yes," Richards responds with a bit of a snicker. "Targeting ground units." He shakes his head as much as the equipment surrounding him will allow. "We're really going to have to check these communications."

Captain Richards unleashes the metallic hatred on the military base. The prototype is angled for a long strafing run. First, he targets the exposed vehicles and people on one of the long runways that splinter from the command center. Then, slowly, his targeting rises to the command center itself. Finally, he fires all forms of death, from bullets to explosives, to energy weapons.

"Disengage, pilot! Disengage!" The Colonel's words go unheeded.

Captain Richards does not cease his fire or pull out of his descent. His trajectory falls just short of the command center. Instead, he continues to spray a steady stream of destructive rain on the doorstep of the command center.

Survivors of the onslaught scramble throughout the exterior of the base, trying to mount their vehicles and defend themselves.

Richards focuses his fire on the Aeronautical prototypes. People caught in the fire are torn to tattered shreds by the heavy weaponry. Explosive rounds rip through military vehicles, which explode, spewing burning fuel and toxic chemicals in all directions.

Richards focuses his sites on the command center. The automated guns have finished reloading and are prepared to unleash another emotionless wave of rage on his targets.

Bullets pierce through the walls of the command center, ripping through the people inside. Screams and cries intermingle as people desperately seek sanctuary from the onslaught.

With super-heated plasma turning flesh into soup around him, Colonel Anders stands as a statue on his podium in the command center. He appears to be without a care in the world. The serene expression returned to his face.

Colonel Patrick Anders starts to chuckle. Slowly, at first, his quiet amusement gradually increases.

Samantha weaves through the projectiles on her way to the exit. The Colonel's laughter disturbs her. She can feel her heart thudding speedily in her chest. Then, terrified by smoke and screams, she ducks behind objects and slides between panicking station workers. Her hands and knees are covered in the blood of the Captain's victims.

Barely escaping the slaughter, Samantha exits the wounded building. But, before leaving, she glances back to be horrified by Anders, who still stands on his platform, laughing hysterically.

The last of the exoskeleton's rounds pierce through the command center. Then, finally, the exoskeleton crashes to the ground. It rolls several times, then skids to a halt just outside the entrance.

Samantha Shaw hides behind crates of equipment but subconsciously pokes her head out to watch.

Military personnel surround the exoskeleton. Captain Richards is no longer a pilot in their experiment; instead, he is an enemy combatant.

Soldiers flinch with fear when the chest plate opens.

Captain Richards appears from the cockpit, holding a gun in one hand.

"Put it down! Now!" The military police scream with feigned courage.

Captain Richards nonchalantly waves to the crowd, seemingly, without recollecting what just happened or what he's just done. "Hey, everybody." He says joyfully. "Great job on the test! Can't wait to celebrate."

Mark emerges from the crowd. He wears a horrified expression on his bleeding face.

Richards greets his friend with a genuine smile. "Oh, hey, Mark." Richards motions back to the exoskeleton, "looks like drinks are on me."

He sees Samantha emerge from the cargo crates. She is shivering with terror. "Hey, Samantha." He waves happily. "I don't want to die."

Captain Douglas Richards puts the gun to his head and pulls the trigger in one motion. His brains spray pink mist that settles across the ground.

"No!!" Mark isn't thinking straight. He runs to his friend as the body falls lifelessly to the ground.

The corpse of Captain Richards suddenly raises the weapon from the ground and fires. The first shots tear through Mark's chest, killing him. The next rounds, fired randomly, target people in the crowd.

The military police respond by firing thousands of rounds at the already dead body, shredding it to pieces with their gunfire. They continue until their weapons click with the sound of empty magazines.

A shaky voice sounds from the crowd. "What the hell is going on?"

8

In the highest reaches of the Advancement Industries building, above the precious domiciles of the elite, is the office of the most successful chairman of any corporation. This man has been the focus of books, articles, fandom, dissertations, and biographies. He is the greatest prodigy ever to join the ranks of the corporate elite. And yet, so little is known about him. He is an enigma. An apparition to those who serve him. And this is for a good reason.

Immobilized by the final stages of ALS, Christian Drake sits in his incredibly sophisticated chair. This magnificent piece of equipment is more than some simple wheelchair; instead, it is an extension of his body, responding to his every thought with robotic precision. Connected to the rest of his office, his chair can communicate his complex commands to every inch of his surroundings.

Christian Drake needs this to be true. His debilitating disease has taken everything from him. He cannot move anything but his eyes; he is a slave to the technology that frees him. Hundreds of monitors display countless events throughout the city. His eyes scan back and forth, watching every event.

Hidden in the safe confines of the tower, Drake can see everything that happens in the world without touching it. He has become an enigma to the world and it to him. Hardly anyone has ever met him. He makes sure of that. Heads of companies are meant to be seen as human perfection. Drake cannot allow people to see his degradation. It would undermine his authority. His attention focuses on the failed experiment. He watches the last of the carnage before activating communication with his assistant.

Christian Drake sends the message, acting as his voice. It simply states. "Wake him up."

Not long after his order is received, it is executed.

Somewhere in the city of Chamariko, inside a dark facility hidden away from public awareness, the eyes of Johnny Vinz flutter open.

His body is stretched across a gurney. Restraints attached to the railing on either side of his poorly cushioned bedding hang uselessly over the cream-colored tile floor. The world surrounding him is fuzzy. Nothing but blurry silhouettes can be seen.

The blurry silhouette of a doctor can be seen against the hospital lighting.

"Welcome back." The doctor greets him as he gently touches Johnny's chest. "Don't try to move just yet. You need to let yourself get acclimated."

His image slowly comes into focus. He is a youthful man with a vibrant energy that seems to beam from his eyes. Light brown hair waves across his head. And a small, tightly manicured Freddy Mercury mustache holds tightly to his upper lip. But, all in all, he looks like a dork.

Though he can't move anything except for his eyes, Johnny Vinz is clearly having considerable trouble breathing. Fear settles into his gaze. He can neither sit up nor move, even without the restraints to hold him to the gurney. They may have been attached to his body at one time, but not now.

"Don't try to talk. I know; your lungs feel on fire every time you inhale. Just keep breathing. The pain will subside along with the rest of your symptoms." The doctor's voice is calm, soothing, and trustworthy.

Johnny Vinz stares at the doctor. His expression is a blend of fear and confusion.

The doctor monitors him closely. "Can you blink?" He can blink, it is challenging, but he can do it.

"Okay. Blink once for no and twice for yes. Do you understand?"

Johnny blinks twice.

"Do you remember me?"

One blink.

"Do you know where you are?"

One blink.

"Do you remember your name?"

One blink.

The doctor sighs. "Okay. What you are experiencing is acute anterograde amnesia brought on by your surgery. Luckily, this is a condition that will pass. The hardware used in your brain tissue needs to make a cognitive connection. This takes time. Unfortunately, we cannot continue with your activation until you've registered your memories."

If he had control of his eyebrows, Johnny Vinz would wrinkle them.

"Force yourself to remember who you are, and your memories should be triggered like a spiderweb."

This does nothing to aid in his understanding of his situation.

"What do you remember?"

Vinz widens his eyes in a moment of fear.

"What is your name?"

Johnny Vinz endeavors to remember. It comes with incredible difficulty. But, in one moment, he suddenly finds himself in his mind. His eyes suddenly flash with recollection. He looks back at the doctor with a confident gaze.

"You found the web."

Two blinks.

"Do you remember your name?"

Two blinks.

"You remember everything?"

Two blinks.

The doctor nods and then scribbles a note into his file.

"Okay. The easy step is over. Now that your memory lock is done, you need to move. You're going through so much pain because the system simultaneously reads and calibrates to your mind-body connection. Your mind needs to re-remember everything about your body, including its pain thresh-hold in each individual muscle, bone, and joint. Having said that, we should take this one step at a time. Can you say your name?"

Johnny Vinz opens his mouth, but only a pathetic whimper squeaks out of his lips.

"Good." The doctor continues scribbling in his file. "Wow, I didn't expect you to be able to make a sound so quickly. You're doing great."

With a sudden jolt, Johnny lifts himself up. His face is frozen in a horrific expression of pain. He screams in agonizing spasms. Each movement draws him closer to a sitting position. "My-name-is-Johnny-Vinz!"

Johnny is now sitting on his bed. With a face drenched in sweat and pale as a ghost, his feet dangle just above the floor.

He sees his reflection in the glass of a window set in the wall on the other side of the room. He might have been called African-American at one time. But America does not exist anymore. Neither does Africa, for that matter. Only Chamariko and an unknown number of cities live in the vast wasteland. No one knows how many cities there are because no one has ever survived a quest into the boundless nothingness beyond the borders of their home.

Johnny Vinz looks into the dark brown eyes of his reflection. Dark eyes, dark skin, and dark hair. The hair may be short, but it is already beginning to curl in on itself, creating a mini-Afro. His physique could be more impressive. Not flabby, but not hardened either. Overall, Johnny Vinz looks like an average, run-of-the-mill guy.

The doctor raises his hands in concern, ready to support Vinz if he falls. "You trying to win a record? You need to slow down."

"All this pain is mental, right? There is nothing physically wrong with me?" Johnny might be asking for clarification, but the clarification is mainly for the doctor's peace of mind and not his own.

"Well," the doctor's words stumble out of his mouth. "It's not physical, but the pain is still real."

"Then I'm standing on my feet."

Screaming in pain the whole time, Johnny Vinz hops off the bed and collapses to his hands and knees. He breathes in deep, exhausted breaths. He speaks one word with each gasping breath. "Really-takes-a-lot-out-of-you."

The doctor shakes his head in amazement. "It is beyond remarkable how quickly you are recuperating. Reteaching people's motor skills is usually an incredibly long and difficult process."

"Trust me, doc, this is ain't easy."

Johnny stands with considerably less difficulty. His steps are taken with increasing ease.

The doctor scribbles more notes in his file as he monitors Johnny.

"Looks like your brain enhancements are calibrated to your physical signals."

Johnny Vinz nods. "Let's never do that again."

The doctor laughs. "You will never have to." He stops himself. "I don't think."

A haze of woozy sensations overwhelms Johnny Vinz. He puts his hand over his eyes and falls back against his bed.

He no longer sees through the basic vision that everyone in the world enjoys. Now, he sees every spectrum of light. Data pings off every electronic device throughout the horizon. Radio waves bleed through the walls. Even the sound vibrations of people walking in the hallway can be seen in his vision. The amount of information is staggering.

"What the hell?" Johnny says, sliding down to the floor.

The doctor nods. "...and now you're connected to the network."

Vinz is too discombobulated to understand the doctor; still, he tries. "My eyes are connected to the wireless network?"

"No," the doctor responds, "your brain is."

He slowly regains his balance. But the multitude of visuals is still overwhelming. He sees the radar ping of electronics, the heat signatures of people, scents floating through the air, and so much more. "My eyes."

"Oh, yes." The doctor produces a set of augmented glasses. "These should help you filter out the information."

The glasses wrap around Johnny's head. Effectively covering the entirety of his vision.

It works.

Johnny Vinz no longer feels overwhelmed by the visual extravaganza he'd endured a moment ago.

"Now what?" He is ready for the next step.

The doctor rolls an advanced computer across the room and sets it against the wall. "I want you, from there, to turn on and hack into this computer. Then tell me what's in the secured file."

Vinz stares at the computer's optical input port.

It is the most logical access point. Johnny Vinz thinks. He focuses on that small port. It may have been designed for physical access, but something in him leads Johnny Vinz to believe that he can see straight into the computer's programming through the wires of that input port. And it works. He remotely activates the machine.

The computer hums to life. He takes another moment to access the secure files hidden within its electronic confines.

He reads the file aloud. "Christian Drake."

"You have a meeting with him as soon as I clear you.

Johnny nods. "When do you clear me?"

"I just did."

"The elevators are over there, right?"

The doctor smiles. "Yes. Elevators are out the door and to the left. I'm sure you'll figure out where to go from there."

9

Samantha Shaw sits in a cold interrogation room. It has become increasingly brisk as she's been here. This is by design. Protocol dictates that the room becomes steadily less comfortable during the interrogation process. And she has been in this interrogation room for quite some time.

She is cold, and tired from the incessant questioning. Dark circles have formed under her eyes, and she wears a haggard expression.

Sitting across from her, the interrogator stares at her with an expression more chilly than the room. Her discomfort is reaching a fever pitch. But, at least her hands stopped shaking. The adrenaline continued pumping long after the incident ended.

It's hard seeing that much carnage without breaking down. Ms. Shaw doesn't know how soldiers can compartmentalize such terrible experiences. They walk around as if nothing affected them. It is only when soldiers do things like Captain Douglas Richards at the military complex that one realizes they are affected by the carnage surrounding them.

Her hands are clasped in her lap. Partially for warmth and partly to calm her nerves. Her body is painfully tight, not from fear but from frustration. Samantha entertained the thought that Colonel Anders had tried to throw her under the bus for quite some time.

The man sitting across from her with an icy stare is a detective. These are dangerous individuals to sit across from in any situation. They are trained to get results. His sole purpose is convincing a suspect of their guilt.

The detective appeared gentler when their conversation began, but that facade wore off quickly as his intentions became clear. The military needs the fault of this debacle to lay with a single individual. Something they can put into news reports to reassure the commonwealth that matters are resolved.

He waits for Samantha to shift uncomfortably before speaking. "Let's go over this again, shall we?"

Samantha rubs her face in frustration and sighs.

The detective doesn't notice, or he just doesn't care. "For all this time, Captain Douglas Richards showed no signs of a psychotic break."

"He showed signs." She corrects.

"Signs that were never cataloged."

"Yes, they were." She corrects again.

"By which physician?"

She eyes him with burning intensity. "All of the physicians recorded irregularities, but none identified it."

"But you did."

She doesn't look away. Better to attack this questioning head-on, as she's been doing. "Yes."

"When?"

"Moments before the incident." *How many times do I have to answer the same questions?* She knows the answer to her own question, as many times as it takes to get a confession.

"And you didn't say anything?" *There it is. My fault.* It has to be someone's fault. So, it has to be hers.

"I told the Colonel, but he was too busy laughing like a lunatic while everyone was..." She trails off, remembering the horrific event. It feels like PTSD. She's never experienced this before.

But she remembers studying it. It feels worse than they described.

"What did you say to Colonel Patrick Anders?"

"Something is wrong."

"That's it?" He is still trying to make it her fault.

If anyone is at fault, she thinks, *it's the Colonel. Or maybe, it was that idiot representative from Advancement Industries who pressured me to proceed with the experiment.*

The detective notices her silence and continues with his questioning. "What did you notice about Captain Douglas Richards?"

She drops her head on the table. She is so tired of answering the same questions over and over. "I told you already."

"Tell me again."

"I noticed a constant irregularity that exposed itself sporadically and without provocation.

After a great deal of analysis, I found a connection between the irregularities." *Hopefully, my answer has enough big words for him to believe me.* But that's not his job; she knows this. His career is investigating and attributing blame.

"What connection? How did you find it?"

"When his system was engaged with the prototype, it registered his heartbeat and sent that back to our records. But the nano-machines we ran through Richards' body were also sending us his vitals." This is not Samantha's answer; it's the setup.

"And they didn't match?"

"At first," she continues, "that's what I noticed. But there was something else."

"Besides Captain Douglas Richards opening fire on the facility?" That was a jab, not an honest question. He is trying to evoke emotion and get her to slip up.

"I told you, the Captain didn't do anything."

The detective might have laughed if he was allowed to show human emotion. This is his job. He keeps emotions out of this interrogation room. The subjects of his investigations never have an ally in this room. "There is a lot of evidence to contradict your statement."

"Like the fact that a dead man could open fire on a crowd of people?" Samantha blurts out unconsciously. She wishes she hadn't. It makes her appear crazy. Any misstep will make her the villain of this debacle.

"He did it. Captain Douglas Richards was a fully functioning asset to our industry before he spoke to you."

There it is again. Will I ever be free of suspicion?

"Excuse me?" Samantha asks in an indignant tone. She cast an exasperated expression, but internally, she knew this was coming.

Her righteous indignation compels her to leap across the table and strangle this pencil pusher. Fortunately, she resists the urge.

"Three weeks after speaking with you, a trained pilot, with nary a traffic ticket, took it upon himself to open fire on his own people, killing dozens and wounding twice as many." Samantha doesn't even try to stop her mouth from running. "The Captain was dead when he pulled the trigger, and I would venture to say that he'd been dead for a long time before I spoke with him."

Now, the detective scoffs. A flash of emotion. He won't let it happen again. "Captain Douglas Richards, a real-life dead man walking, you say. Except that his heart was checked constantly."

"But not his brain chemistry. At least, not with the correct sensors. He had some particular flat lines throughout the sensors. I need to see the report." She is entitled to this. These days, reading a report is like facing your accuser.

"Once we've finished." Technically, he does not have the authority to deny her request. But he wants his confession.

Samantha leans forward. "We have finished. There are only so many ways that I can tell you the same thing."

The detective ignores her. "If no sensor showed how the specific brain death in Captain Douglas Richards occurred, how did you figure it out?"

It is tricky responding to questions when no one wants to hear the answer. It is even more complicated when the answer is so obscure.

"He kept making side comments. Things that you might be able to pass off individually, but after a while, I found a pattern."

The detective is perplexed. "Okay, let's go back to the beginning."

Samantha shakes her head. *He is like a broken record.* She thinks to herself. Finally, Samantha Shaw realizes she needs to do something different to get off this merry-go-round.

"Who is Vinz?" She asks.

Now Samantha has the detective on the defensive. "What?"

Samantha might just have the one to blame. And she is not going to miss this opportunity. "The Captain said that name had something to do with this. Ask him."

"Who, or what, is Vinz? Why would Captain Douglas Richards mention him? Nothing in any of the files that refer to that name." The detective is genuinely intrigued.

"Nor in mine."

"So, what does he have to do with this?"

No answer is given. There is no time for an answer. The door opens, and an executive from Advancement Industries briskly walks into the room. He whispers something intelligible into the detective's ear.

Of course, Advancement Industries was listening. She restrains herself from speaking aloud. *They listen to everything.*

The detective is not amused, dismayed, or uncomfortable. Instead, he glances at Samantha, gathers his papers, and says, "You're free to go."

"What?" Samantha doesn't want to look a gift horse in the mouth, but she feels more infuriated now than when she was interrogated. She wants an answer to her question. *Who is Vinz?*

"A car is waiting for you outside. Have a nice day." The detective finishes gathering his things and leaves.

Samantha's departure from this uncomfortable situation is incredibly confusing. She stands from the hardened aluminum chair and exits the chilly interrogation room. A wall of warm air welcomes her as she makes her way through the Department of Investigations building, and, as expected, she sees a car that waits to transport her to another conflict. She almost expected to leave the building and be greeted by a firing squad. Or to be dosed discreetly with some fatal concoction.

As it is, the reality is more mundane than the imagination, although, in this case, significantly more cryptic. A representative of Advancement Industries waits for her in a high-class sedan, holding the rear door open.

"Samantha?" The representative greets. He should have been holding up a sign.

"Yes." She responds.

"Could you come with me, please?" He says while motioning to the interior of the car.

"Who are you?" It's a stupid question to ask. She already knows who he is. He's a company representative making her life a living hell.

"I'm a representative of Advancement Industries." He responds with a welcoming smile. "Everything will be explained in the car. This way, please." He enters the vehicle behind her and closes the door. She feels a gentle jolt as the driverless car embarks toward its destination. The atmosphere inside this elegant vehicle is delightful compared to the world outside. Samantha can feel her body slowly relax. Ambient music plays quietly as the car moves through traffic.

The representative produces an electronic tablet. Samantha knows what this means. She accepts the tablet.

"Before we continue," he begins, "I need to clarify that anything and everything you see and hear is not to travel beyond the people involved. Do you understand?" He not only needs her acknowledgment, but he also needs her signature.

Samantha glances down at the information presented on the tablet. A standard non-disclosure agreement. Complete with terrifying ramifications if she breaks it. If there is one thing that Advancement Industries is good at, it's destroying anyone who crosses the company.

"Please sign with an eye print to confirm your acknowledgment." The representative gently reminds her.

There was a time that people used hand signatures. They were forged. Then fingerprints were used. Those were developed as well. It would only be a matter of time before people found a way to fabricate a rental scan.

Once Samantha scans her eye, the representative continues with his presentation. "I represent Mr. Drake."

Samantha can feel a shock in her body. Then, it is a wave of tension that slowly settles.

"Christian Drake of Advancement Industries?" This is the surprise of a lifetime. Christian Drake is one of the titans of Chamariko. His innovation, direction, and presence are why Advancement Industries is the excellent institution that people have come to rely upon; yet, he is an enigma, a real 'King of Babylon' type. When he spoke, the world moved without question and in agreement. No command was challenged. No decision was rejected. Not after his guidance outlasted the leadership of John Demure of Trans-Production Incorporated.

Everyone does what he says, no matter what. And the craziest thing is, hardly anyone has met him. Some years ago, Drake retreated into the confines of his penthouse on the top floor of the Advancement Industries tower. Maybe, two people have seen him since.

"What does he want with me?" Samantha believes in herself but is hardly among the top five most influential people in Chimariko.

The representative acknowledges her surprise with a nod. "What you experienced was not an isolated incident."

She always knew they watched everything. Samantha is unsure what scares her more: this has happened elsewhere in the city or that no one has heard about it. "What do you mean?"

"That information is not the reason for this conversation."

They are always compartmentalizing. Samantha Shaw thinks to herself.

"Before we continue," the representative begins again.

This again? He is giving me another verbal warning. It's more legal documentation. *They must be getting ready to show me something vital to Advancement Industries.*

"It needs to be made perfectly clear that anything you divulge from this moment forward will be considered a breach of contract. You understand what that means?"

Fire and Brimstone. "Yes." She responds. *Whatever is going on must be making them extremely nervous.*

"Good. Though not public knowledge, Mr. Drake has suffered from a genetic disease crippling his entire body. He has been affected by this disease for some time now."

"Oh, my God." Samantha doesn't know why the representative shares this information, but this seems like a perfectly reasonable response.

"The only reason I tell you this is that Mr. Drake's time is precious. So, needless to say, he doesn't like wasting time allowing people to get acclimated to his appearance." But, of course, this could be considered vanity in any other situation.

Samantha nods. "I think I get it."

"Do you?" His tone is intimidating.

"He isn't self-conscious; he just doesn't want to waste time discussing it."

A smile. *So the representative is human, after all.* "I'm happy that you understand." He leans his head back on the headrest like he just powered down. The car isn't moving anymore. They must have reached their destination.

Samantha glances out of the vehicle window. She sees the artistic design of the Advancement Industries tower. This is her dream. To be called to the 'corporate cul-de-sac' and enter one of the incredible buildings in the intersection.

She marvels at the masterful artistry of the building. Such incredible attention to every detail of the tower's entrance instills a sense of control and authority. Yet, in all her efforts to be considered 'elite', Samantha has never found herself so close to the hub of 'corporate cul-de-sac'. It is even more intimidating than she believed.

Elites and representatives move like ants as they pass by each other in rotating doors. Each one has more societal authority than Ms. Shaw could dream. She feels her body tighten with anxiety.

Samantha Shaw knows it's time to exit the vehicle and make the vertical journey to Drake's office, but intimidation urges her to hesitate.

"Have..." the fear forces her to stumble over her words. "Have you met Mr. Drake personally?" She says while lightly tucking her blonde hair behind her round ear. Her fingers gently squeeze her free earlobe as she brings her hand down to her side.

He says nothing.

"I visited Advancement Industries once when I was a little girl." She stares at the building with the same expression that she wore as a young child. It's incredible how such a daunting display of authority can regress someone back to their youth.

The representative appears frustrated. Samantha doesn't understand why she's trying to make small talk. Perhaps she's just trying to stall and work up the nerve for her meeting with the most dominant individual in Chamariko. "The most powerful company on the planet. And connection point to-"

"Not to be rude," the representative cuts her off. "But there is no legal or contractual reason for us to speak further in this vehicle."

Samantha tries to hide her embarrassment. "Okay." *Such an odd thing to say, 'legal or contractual'. These Advancement Industry types are so strange.*

The young computer analyst stands outside the entrance of the gaudy building. The doors never seem to stop moving. They constantly give way to executives entering and leaving the building for various reasons. She can feel her heart trying to break through her chest. The thumping pushes against her ribs like a rhythmic drum beat.

The skyscraper directly across from the four-lane street bustling with traffic houses the most significant rival to Advancement Industries. A giant titanium statue of their late leader stands proudly halfway between the road and the building. It is a statue of John Demure. The corporate nemesis Christian Drake ever faced in his tenure at Advancement Industries, though, many speculated a close working relationship developed between the two near the end of Demure's life. Above the statue, several stories from the ground floor, the company's name, "Transproduction Incorporated," is displayed in arrogantly large letters. Where Advancement Industries focused its resources on advancing hardware, Trans-Production Incorporated rested its reputation on genetics and biology.

Further down the corporate cul-de-sac lay the last three skyscrapers. Mockingly called the children of the corporate monoliths, these companies filled the different needs of the people of Chamariko.

Samantha finally gathers enough strength to enter the Advancement Industries headquarters through the entrance's thick glass doors.

"Welcome to Advancement Industries." The pleasing sound of a synthetic voice greets Samantha as she enters the building. "Hello, my name is Alon, and I am the 'All Information' kiosk of Advancement Industries. My purpose is to assist you in navigating through this expansive corporate building. With my extensive knowledge of the building's layout and personnel, I can help you find your way or locate the correct representative.

"I also possess a vast database of intriguing facts about our corporation and the building itself. If you have any questions or are curious about anything related to Advancement Industries, feel free to ask me, and I will provide you with all the information you need.

"Please don't hesitate to reach out to me if you require any assistance or have any concerns. It is my pleasure to help you in any way that I can. How may I assist you today, valued user?"

I wonder if it is true? Samantha wonders as she stares at the petite, glass-gall-colored holographic avatar on a platform before her. Supposedly, the founder of Advancement Industries modeled the avatar after his dead teenage daughter. Samantha only allows the thought to linger momentarily before making her request.

"I'm here to meet with Christian Drake." She says with a little shake in her voice.

"Certainly, I'd be happy to assist you with that. Mr. Drake's office is located on the top floor of this building. If you have an appointment with him, you can proceed directly to his office. If not, I can assist you with scheduling a meeting or connecting you with another executive who may be able to assist you further." Alon responds pleasantly. "Please let me know how I can assist you in this matter. "

"Yes, I have a meeting scheduled with Mr. Drake. My name is Samantha Shaw."

"Thank you for informing me, Samantha Shaw. Before proceeding to Mr. Drake's office on the top floor, I must ask you to first retrieve a security pass at the security desk located near the entrance. Once you have your pass, please make your way to the elevators found in the corner of the lobby behind the security desk." Alon responds in her agreeable tone. "The elevators will take you directly to the top floor, where Mr. Drake's office is located. If you need any assistance, the security personnel at the desk will be happy to help you. "

"I hope you have a productive meeting with Mr. Drake! If there's anything else I can do to assist you, please let me know."

"No, thank you," Samantha says with a shake.

"Certainly! Thank you for using my services, I hope your experience was satisfactory. If you have any other questions, feel free to visit any of my kiosks located throughout the building. Before we part ways, I'd like to remind you of our company slogan: Always succeeding, always advancing. It represents our commitment to excellence and innovation in all that we do here at Advancement Industries. Thank you for choosing us, and we look forward to continuing to serve you. Have a great day!"

Samantha moves to the security station. Thankfully, the short virtual conversation was enough to calm her nerves. It is not every day that you get to meet the King of Babylon.

10

Gadgets and computer systems cover the desk of Christian Drake. They are his router to the world outside of his penthouse. They are his lifeline to society.

Too much of the world, this tower is a monument to the authority of Advancement Industries. To him, it is a home, an office, and a hospital. Not a prison, though. That is a definition used for his body. A broken-down hunk of flesh with no real purpose but to store his consciousness.

Christian Drake laments his position every day of his life. He was once a great man. Now he is a terrifying shadow. His eyes shift from screen to screen. The disease took nearly everything from him, but it left his vision. He is thankful for that.

The screens do not line a wall; they fill his office. Constantly flickering between security cameras, military recorders, and news outlets faster than any ordinary human being could comprehend. If not for his augmentations, Drake would not be capable of understanding the amount of information either. This steady stream of information quenches his thirst for the outside world, a waterfall of knowledge. It is his only connection point.

Many of his most difficult decisions have already been made. Leading up to the activation of the Vinz project, he's had to contend with social disorder, rival corporations, and sycophantic believers of dead and outdated belief systems. Finally, he is about to find out how successful his legacy will be.

Drake's gaze stops on an image of Samantha, timidly making her way through the Advancement Industries' lobby. The screen doesn't flicker and doesn't shift to a different monitor; instead, it holds focus on Samantha's meek journey to the security station. The computer knows where his attention lies. He designed it that way. A direct connection from his brain to the processor ensures that he never misses a moment he wishes to maintain in his focus.

His office shifts. Once a bastion of technology, the domicile transforms into an extravagant display of luxury. Christian Drake feels this atmosphere will be the most disarming for Samantha. He needs her to be calm. Christian Drake needs her to be accepting. Because he needs her help.

Samantha signs in with a rental scan. She can feel her heart trying to break out of her chest. If it beats any harder, it may explode.

She is quickly escorted to an elevator nestled in the corner of the lobby.

When the elevator doors open again, Samantha is exposed to Christian Drake's elegant office. The office displays incredible art from the greatest of artists in Chamariko. Marbling on the floor guides her on a pathway to Drake's desk.

She is dumbfounded by the mass amount of information that surrounds her. The technology is far beyond anything that she's seen in her life. And yet, without her awareness, it is a semblance of his office's genuine innovations.

Overwhelming her was not his intention. Christian Drake has been surrounded by the most advanced technology in the world for so long that he's lost the awareness of what typical people are used to seeing. Still, it's less intimidating than before he altered it.

The elevator doors close behind her. The thud of their shutting reminds Samantha that she is alone in a room with the most powerful man in the world. She's suddenly grateful that the representative shared Christian Drake's condition. She's not sure how many surprises she could handle in one moment. Still, there's more to come.

Christian Drake's chair is turned away from Samantha. All she sees are the wires coming out of its back.

"Mr. Drake?" Her voice comes out meeker than Samantha anticipated. She slowly walks into the center of the elegant office, following the guidance of the marble flooring. "I was told you wanted a meeting with me?" She wishes she could muster more than a mousy voice when speaking to him. But, unfortunately, her nerves make this impossible.

"Welcome to my office." These are Christian Drake's words, but not his voice. Instead, an automated voice system communicates with him. His speech is just another ability that this decrepit disease stole from him.

The chair turns, and Samantha sees Christian Drake for the first time.

"Um," she stumbles over her words momentarily, her tongue tightening into knots. Drake is used to this. "You wanted to speak to me?"

"Yes. Please, have a seat." Christian Drake's automated voice changes to a more casual tone. "Would you like anything to drink? Water? Coffee?"

"Nothing to drink, thank you. I just want answers." She says as boldly as she is capable of expressing.

"You and me both." His agreement confuses Ms. Shaw. Reality is seldom matched to the imagination, and in her dream, Christian Drake knows everything.

Samantha sits in a comfortable chair on the opposite side of Christian Drake's desk. "I'm sorry?"

"Who is Vinz?"

Is he repeating what I said? She wonders. *Or is he just asking?* "I don't know."

"You mentioned him several times during your debriefing."

Debriefing is such an altruistic way to describe my interrogation. "It felt more like an interrogation." She needs this to be explicit.

"Your overzealous debriefing." Christian Drake corrects.

"The Captain dreamed about Vinz several times before his episode." The episode is another charming description of a hellish event. "I'm trying to figure out what this Vinz has to do with the experiment."

"Nothing."

He knows who Vinz is. Perhaps Christian Drake knows more than he is letting on. "Then what went wrong?" She asks, furrowing her eyebrows.

"Nothing went wrong with the experiment. And there is no Vinz affiliated with your project."

This conversation is becoming more confusing with each passing moment. Samantha Shaw tries to shake the confusion out of her mind.

"What?"

Part of the wall transforms into a television. Samantha leans back in her chair, struck by the technology. She's never heard of material that could reconstruct itself at will. Let alone witness it.

The television shows a news report of a psychotic man killing innocent people at random. He stands in the middle of the street as terrified pedestrians run for cover. The man screams and laughs hysterically and screams gibberish with each shot.

Why does he look so familiar? Ms. Shaw thinks to herself as she watches the horrifying images on the screen. She stares at the figure curiously but does not realize why she has this sensation until Christian Drake speaks.

"For some time now, our firewalls have been engaged with..." Christian Drake's robotic voice seems to search for the right words, "a virus of sorts."

"I don't understand." Samantha hates repeating herself, but nothing in this conversation makes sense, and this conversation doesn't seem to alleviate her confusion. "I told the Colonel-" a sudden realization stops her mid-sentence. *The psychotic,* she realizes, *the gunman is Colonel Patrick Anders!* When met with the police force, the degraded psychopath commits suicide. Flashes of Captain Douglas Richards stick in Samantha's mind.

"Colonel Patrick Anders, it seems, was infected by this virus for quite a while longer than Captain Douglas Richards."

Samantha Shaw twists her mouth as she finally starts to understand. "So, the test wasn't for the suit?" This is a statement masquerading as a question.

"How did you know something was wrong? Do you have any upgrades?"

"No," Samantha responds, shaking her head. "I'm one hundred percent organic." Christian Drake tries to nod his head, but his disability restrains him. "So, you have no connection to server data."

"Analog is not dead." *Despite the common belief,* she thinks to herself, her eyes unable to break from the nightmarish images, *some people still prefer to be organic.*

"No." Christian Drake admits. "Just inefficient."

Samantha can't take her eyes off the television screen. She watches the corpse re-animate and continue killing innocent people until a barrage of bullets tears the body to pieces. Then, the images cut off abruptly.

"Efficiency isn't everything," Samantha responds, her eyes still fixated on the screen. "I noticed a discrepancy. His vital signs were perfectly within range." It sounds crazy, even to her.

"You knew he was dying by how healthy he was?" Strangely, the computer acting as the voice for the chief executive officer of Advancement Industries seems confused by this. At least, that is the tone the automated voice appears to take.

Samantha turns her gaze to Christian Drake. This is her moment to defend herself. "His vital signs were perfect. I mean, perfect. Every fluctuation, every change that the monitors picked up from his body were textbook variations. No one's body is perfectly within range all the time. Not even the augmented."

Christian Drake would nod if his body permitted it. "So, you realized that while every monitor saw him as alive-"

"That he was actually dead. Yes."

Samantha can see Christian Drake's understanding, even through his debilitating disease.

"Interesting."

She's starting to feel emboldened. "Furthermore, I believe when the Captain was dreaming about this Vinz character, he was already dead. There is no Vinz anywhere. I checked." "The very fact that Captain Richards mentioned his name is concerning." Christian Drake appears to be opening up.

Is he an ally? Samantha is still worried that security officers are waiting at the elevator doors to take her to some prison that doesn't exist on any record.

"When you mentioned it during your... interrogation, I called you here."

"Why?" Even if she gets taken away, she'll get some answers in this room.

"Vinz." Christian Drake begins, "represents a prototype for our next generation technologies. With the success of the Vinz project, we are looking to advance beyond the physical limitations of our organic bodies."

"Vinz is a computer?" Samantha's question is answered when the elevator doors open. As they part, revealing Johnny Vinz. His eyes are hidden behind incredibly sophisticated glasses. Samantha Shaw can almost see the circuitry at the corners of the lenses. Vinz, the brainchild of Advancement Industries, walks confidently into the office with a knowing expression. It is as if he already understands what is happening and why he has been called to Drake's office. His advanced suit does nothing to conceal his sidearms.

"Why don't I have him explain?"

Samantha looks up this new entry into the room. A thin man with ebony skin. He is far less muscular than Captain Richards, and if he is as augmented as he was, he seems to hide those enhancements inside his body.

Johnny Vinz nods. "I have billions of cell-sized machines flowing through my body connected directly to my nervous system."

Samantha speaks to Drake. She clearly is having trouble comprehending all that she is experiencing. "You fused the human nervous system with an electronic one?"

"My greatest creation." There is pride in his statement. "The world's strongest human and the world's smartest computer in one place. If he were to be infected, he would know." Christian Drake turns his attention to Johnny Vinz. Or, more specifically, his eyes focus on him. "My firewalls are falling at an exponential rate. If this continues, we could lose the global mainframe within a year."

"Why is she here?" Johnny Vinz disregards Samantha's presence for a moment.

"I need to investigate the cause of this system malfunction. I need to know what is causing this and why."

"You don't know?" Johnny Vinz drops his jaw, almost mimicking the same flabbergasted expression as Samantha. "I thought you could see everything."

"It takes time for water to reach a waterfall. Just as it takes time for information to come to me." Drake answers.

"But you're afraid the waterfall will be poisoned before you find the contaminant." Vinz completes Drake's metaphor.

Christian Drake flashes another expression of acknowledgment. "To continue my analogy, yes. My firewalls are still operational, but I can't be sure for how long. Military and off-grid programs are infected. Soon, it will be the infrastructure of the entire city."

"If the city is infected with some virus," Samantha butts in, "why doesn't anyone know? Why isn't there a quarantine in effect?"

"The outbursts are random throughout the entire city." Christian Drake answers. "We could all be infected and not even realize it."

The very thought makes Samantha shutter. *An infection that broke quarantine before one could be initiated. It would be the end of civilization.*

"Why is she here?" Johnny Vinz repeats his question.

"Samantha is organic." Christian Drake answers, his chair shifting back and forth between the two.

Johnny Vinz nods.

What does that have to do with anything? Samantha wonders.

"Who or what is the cause of the virus?" Johnny Vinz asks. He is interested to know who wrote the program that crippled the world. The one that could drive fear into the great Christian Drake.

"We don't know." Christian Drake answers ominously.

Johnny Vinz shakes his head, not accepting this answer. "But you have an idea."

Christian Drake pauses before replying. "I can't say."

The two share a look. Samantha feels the hairs on her arm raise on end as the intensity rises in the room.

Christian Drake and Johnny Vinz stare into each other's eyes. Aside from the low hum of electronics, the room is silent.

Just as he'd done in the hospital room, Johnny hacks into Christian Drake's unique computer system through his augmented eyes. Christian Drake lowers his internal firewalls to make the transition effortlessly seamless.

The image of Johnny Vinz is constructed in a computerized construct of Christian Drake's mind. He prepares to continue their conversation in secret. The decrepit old leader of Advancement Industries is nowhere in sight.

Visually, the virtual world appears shifty and wrong. Objects are out of focus, sometimes disconnected from other objects, floating like some ethereal body above and around their intended connection point. The virtual atmosphere is like a glitchy video game.

Johnny Vinz can see an illuminated outline of every object in his surroundings. Every surface in the room is either straight lines or spheres, as if the world is

governed by the laws of sacred geometry. At the center of the room, a sphere glowing with a bluish hue hovers head-high over the floor.

Johnny Vinz scans the room with his augmented eyes. He lightly shifts his head back and forth as he syncs with the electronic nervous system hidden in the confines of Christian Drake's virtual reality. The synthetic environment shutters sporadically as Johnny Vinz' mind finishes adjusting with Christian Drake's. After a few moments, the two are fully connected, and every object locks in place once the buffering is completed. Johnny Vinz now stands in the solid construction of a virtual world. The orb continues to hover in its place.

As Johnny Vinz inspects this virtual place, he feels a strange chill from the cold fireplace.

Approaching the ashy cavern of the wooden wall of the log cabin, he examines the details of the fireplace's brick layout and notices various dots in strategic places. As his eyes set on each of the luminous dots, strange clicking sounds pop inside the walls. As he focuses on the final piece of the poorly hidden combination lock, objects in the room move as if controlled by telepathy. They migrate into the empty space of the sphere in the center of the room.

Everything fits into a single, three-dimensional shape. Johnny recognizes the symbol. It is a symmetrical symbol called the 'flower of life'. The brainchild of

Advancement Industries hears the three-dimensional model click into the ambiguous lock.

The fireplace lights in a flame that produces immense heat. The raging fire grows from the brick fireplace, eventually consuming the cabin. Johnny Vinz is unaffected by his burning surroundings. He slowly comes to the realization that he is not alone. Feeling the strange presence, Johnny Vinz spins around and sees Zayyir reach for his throat.

As he clasps his fingers around Johnny's neck, he screams, "ZAYYIR!!"

The program terminates, and Johnny Vinz feels himself return to reality.

He stands stoically in Christian Drake's office. Ms. Shaw is still in her place, unaware of what has just occurred.

"Thank you." Johnny Vinz says.

These are the first words that Samantha Shaw hears after a long and awkward pause. While these two cyborgs stared at each other, she stood idly in the room without realizing the information that had just transpired between the two. The data being transferred digitally and covertly left no opportunity for prying eyes. Not even the advanced computing system in Drake's office is aware of the transmission.

"You understand the need for secrecy," Drake responds.

Johnny Vinz nods. "Yes, I do." He answers. He flashes a stern look at Samantha. "I'm not responsible for her."

"Understood. She signed the waiver."

Samantha shakes her head, “what waiver.”

“Fill her in, please.” Christian Drake says without looking at her.

Johnny leaves the room, with Samantha following close behind. A baffled expression is smeared across her face.

She wanted answers, but the answers seemed more confusing than the questions.

11

Johnny Vinz exits the Advancement Industries building and enters the 'Corporate cul-de-sac'. The five skyscrapers surround him, including the building he just vacated.

Evening coats the sky with a beautiful orange color. Lights throughout the city are just beginning to warm up. The photosynthetic material illuminates the buildings themselves, but the atmosphere is still too bright to be drowned out by the power of man-made lighting. Just as Thomas Edison sought to make candles obsolete for the average individual, so did the inventor of this incredible material. Strong like concrete and yet, luminous as a light fixture.

The inventor was John Demure. He's dead now. A casualty of the turbulent times of the great transition when governments gave way to a new corporate structure. He guided the movements of 'Trans-Production Incorporated', the second most powerful corporation in the world. Much of his work never saw the light of day, but he was an intricate part of the development of their world nonetheless.

The streets themselves illuminate with the same material. They flag traffic information to alert drivers of oncoming traffic conditions. Accidents plummeted with the implementation of this technology.

Samantha follows Johnny into a black vehicle provided by Advancement Industries. As the car begins moving, he explains the target of their inquiries. Whether the vehicle is driven by autopilot or by Vinz himself, Samantha can't be sure. Neither would surprise her.

"We are searching for the origin of this virus. Drake believes that it was created by Zayyir." Johnny Vinz explains.

"But Zayyir is dead," Samantha says in protest. "He was executed years ago." *So how can we be searching for a corpse?* She ponders. *And how can some dead child be responsible for such a devastating computer virus?*

"So, if he is the cause of the virus..." Johnny Vinz begins.

"...Then that means he released something into the network before the authorities captured him." Samantha feels a shutter crawl up her spine. Her shoulders shake unconsciously as the sensation reaches her neck. "He could have infected the world years ago, and no one would know."

"Because there's no way to confirm who is and is not infected." Johnny Vinz continues. "The entire world would destroy itself through panic." Samantha is unsure if she's more disturbed by the prospect of societal meltdown or by Johnny Vinz' stoic acceptance of such a terrible possibility.

It is clear they are no longer in the refined confines of the 'corporate cul-de-sac'. The atmosphere changes. They are no longer in the magnificent display of corporate society. Instead, Samantha can see the darker urban underground. Removed from the social power of the elites, those living in this land survive at the mercy of their overlords.

Known as the quarantine zone, this part of the city is home to the forgotten souls of Chamariko.

Samantha notices her surroundings. "Where are we?"

"Zayyir's last known cyber armory." Johnny Vinz answers.

"I've never heard of it."

"We entered the quarantined sector." His answer comes just as the car stops. They appear to be just outside of a rinky-dink computer parts shop.

"A computer virus and you bring me to an analog computer parts shop?" Samantha was expecting some extravagant mainframe, large enough to replace a building.

"It was quarantined after Zayyir's capture."

This makes sense to Samantha. Corporate officers captured Zayyir fifteen years ago. She marvels at how much technology grew in fifteen short years. And not just that. How people live as technological cavemen. Samantha may be organic, but even she couldn't fathom living in a world so removed from advancement.

"But if quarantined means off the grid, then how are we supposed to track Zayyir?" Samantha begins.

"There's always a trail," Johnny answers.

"How are we going to find it?" Samantha asks.

They exit the vehicle. Johnny moves for the door. "You do the talking when we go in there. I'll handle the trail."

Samantha nods.

Far removed from the luminous symphony of the 'corporate cul-de-sac', darkness covers the city like a thick curtain. *I can't remember the last time I actually saw the stars.* The young analyst thinks to herself as she stares at a constellation without realizing it.

The exterior of this filthy rundown shop could be more impressive. Small cracks from the lack of attention crawl up the walls from their foundation. The windows are covered with a blackened film. A spider fracture reaches out from the center of one of the windows and touches its four corners. Above a different window, a cheap neon sign attempts to reveal the shop's name. Several letters fail to illuminate, leaving a sign that says 'DO—-R'- MAR-ET'.

Forgotten by most of society, shops like this exist primarily for individuals living on the outskirts of the network. Scandalous individuals seeking to hide from corporate civility live in places like these.

A long dark alleyway trails beyond sight, disappearing in the shadows. Oily dirt covers the asphalt. Along the walls of this filthy corridor, riffraff lies on makeshift bedding consisting of torn blankets scavenged from corporate trash. Samantha Shaw can see a pair of legs poking out from behind a garbage bin. Against one of its walls, Samantha notices graffiti painted onto the brick facade of one of the buildings. One painted message stands out above the rest. It simply states: "Zayyir is coming back. Zayyir will make things right."

Samantha feels a chill crawl up her spine. She never wished to see the dark 'skid-row' type alleyways. But, having seen such a sight, she does not want to see it again.

The shadows move as people with broken cybernetic enhancements slink from one makeshift shelter hidden in the darkness to the next.

"Why do you want me to do the talking? What are you going to do?" Samantha asks, failing to avert her attention from the sleazy alleyway.

Vinz opens the door. "Innovation."

Everything inside the rundown electronics shop could be more appealing. White walls hide behind various trinkets of technology that hang from metal hangers that protrude from the places they've been drilled into. More expensive items sit idly behind wire cages, safe from the thieving fingers of desperate customers. The shop extends like a short hallway to the counter on the opposite side. A single teller sits behind the counter, separated from the rest of the shop by a bulletproof window. A minor groove is cut between the glass and the counter-top to allow for transactions.

The trashy-looking shop owner greets them with a cold stare. The middle-aged man with a receding hairline watches them with a suspicious glare. Strands of hair peel over his exposed scalp in an ill-conceived comb over. They look more like pubic hair on his head with their scraggy curl.

He does not seem embarrassed by this. His clients consist of the desperate. They do not have the time or energy to judge him for his appearance. His gaze remains on the two, sizing them up from behind his thick, bulletproof glass shield. His eyes track them as they migrate to his counter.

"Can you help us?" Samantha asks in the most cordial tone she can muster.

"Probably not." He responds uninterestedly and returns his attention to the trashy magazine.

Samantha is slightly taken aback. She glances at Johnny before continuing. "We're looking for someone."

"I sell equipment, not people."

"We need information, then." The young analyst clarifies.

"I sell equipment, not information." He responds without lifting his attention from the smut on his magazine pages.

Samantha sighs in frustration. "He may have shopped here." She continues.

"If you're not buying something, get out of my shop, cop."

Samantha opens her mouth, ready to spit a venomous retort at the rude shopkeeper. But instead, Johnny steps in, holding a meaningless, universal computer chip. "I just came to buy this."

The menial component carries the emblem of Tinker-Tech, one of the five corporations residing in the corporate cul-de-sac. Many stores in the cede underbelly of Chamariko make use of Tinker-Tech. The company is known for making cheap knockoffs of technology initially designed by Advancement Industries. And building equipment that did not require grid access to operate made trinkets of technology a go-to for the criminal and revolutionary elements of Chamariko.

They would always be more dominant than their high-end, corporate big brother, but Tinker-Tech catered to a clientele and did it well.

Both the shopkeeper and Samantha look at him curiously.

"You're not corporate." The shopkeeper notices aloud.

"Not really." Vinz acknowledges.

"What are you doing with her?" He says, eyeing her with disdain.

Johnny Vinz nods. "Mutual objective. Can I buy this?" He passes a tiny computer chip in the slit between the glass and the counter-top.

The shopkeeper musters a passive smile. "Sure thing."

"You came here to buy something?" Samantha stares at him with a baffled expression.

Johnny Vinz turns to Samantha. "Can you spot me?" He asks.He can't be serious. "What?"

"Come on," Johnny Vinz pleads, "I'm waiting on a check to clear."

Samantha Shaw opens her wallet, revealing a plethora of cards. She fingers a folded cluster of paper credits. "Unbelievable." *This man will be the death of me.* She thinks to herself as she pulls some credits out of her wallet. *I just know it.* With a frustrated sigh, she hands the shopkeeper paper money, a rarity in this day and age. *It might not be as efficient, but there's no way I'm giving this man access to my bank account.*

"Thank you." Vinz smiles. He can feel her frustration and can't help but be amused by it.

As they leave the shop with a broken sign, moving toward their company vehicle, Vinz nonchalantly chucks the piece of technology onto the ground in the alleyway.

Samantha is beside herself. She feels tension rush through her body, seizing her shoulders. "What the hell?!" She exclaims as she gently tucks hair behind her ear, unable to resist the action.

"Zayyir lived a couple dozen miles down that way," Vinz says, paying no mind to her or the recently purchased computer chip. "I have a lead on the source of the virus, but we'll have to search the apartment to get the exact location."

"Wait," Samantha says, shaking her head as if to wiggle the confusion out of her mind.

"How do you know?"

"I couldn't get through his security system without setting off the firewall."

A Trojan horse? "So you used the transaction as a backdoor into his computer system?"

Johnny Vinz nods. "Exactly." He opens the driver's side door. "By the way, I paid your rent."

"I paid for the chip you just threw into the road."

He chuckles. "Not by the time I was done with the transaction." He responds.

Information and thievery? "You hacked in and stole his money?"

Vinz smiles mischievously. "Just what he was skimming. The business is fine."

They get in the car. As their vehicle hums out of sight, a bum stumbles out of the seedy alleyway shadows. One of his arms trembles uncontrollably. He hobbles to the computer chip, his face contorted in intense pain.

He desperately jumps onto the item like a junky onto a needle and tears the wrapping off with his teeth and one good arm. He quickly moves his shirt sleeve, revealing a faulty circuit. Removing a defective chip from his trembling arm, he replaces the useless piece of equipment with the new item discarded by Johnny Vinz.

As soon as the malfunctioning equipment is replaced, he leans back in a blissful haze; his body instantly releasing all of its tension. It is as if blood is flowing back into his arm after days without circulation.

The lights throughout his arm illuminate boldly, and he regains stability. All is well once again.

Suddenly, the shop owner slams the door open, causing another fracture in the building's facade. "You're costing me business!" He screams. "Get off the commercial street, you bum, before I call security."

It's an idle threat. Any rational-thinking individual knows the last thing this shopkeeper needs is security forces investigating his business. It works, though, startling the bum who retreats back into the shadowy confines of the dark alleyway to live with the rest of failed society.

Everyone has a place they belong. And the filthy forgotten streets are where people like this human rat belong. There is no place for compassion in Chamariko.

12

Samantha Shaw stares at Johnny Vinz as they sit in the moving car. She is unsure of how to feel at this particular moment. Having endured so much since that terrible experience at the military base, she is still in a state of shock; Perplexed by the odd range of his abilities, she finds herself lost in a murky haze of fear and intrigue. Not to mention the gnawing Discouragement caused by his lack of concern for the state of humanity. Or, perhaps, she is irked by his stunt in the electronics store. In any case, she has difficulty accepting the current state of things.

The web in her mind blinds her to the change in the atmosphere outside the car. As they left the safe confines of the 'corporate cul-de-sac', they are now falling into the grimy underbelly of Chamariko without her realizing it.

She eventually voices her concerns with a single question. "How are you able to do all of this?"

"I told you, nanotechnology." He responds in a simple tone.

"I've never heard of you before. How long have you been working for Advancement Industries?" In this world, if you did not belong to a corporation, you did not exist in Chamariko, an all-to-real truth for those living in the cede alleyway next to the electronics shop they have just left.

"First off," Vinz begins, "I do not work for Advancement Industries. I am contracted by the corporation to complete a single and specific requirement; we have an agreement, not employment. And, to answer your question. I woke up this morning."

Why does everything have to be so damned confusing? Samantha Shaw wonders as she stares at her mysterious partner. *So I am on a world-saving mission with a newborn baby. I would have hoped for something else. Most cybernetic organisms described their activation as waking up. But Vinz is not a robot. Is he?*

"This morning?" Samantha asks.

"Yup."

Ms. Shaw sinks deep into her chair and stares at nothing. She is lost in the abyss of her own imagination. Her original line of questioning has been derailed with matter-of-fact responses that make no rational sense. *But, no worries,* Samantha thinks as she tries to regain her mental composure; *I must be learning something of value.*

"What was it like?" She inquires, "waking up this morning."

"It sucked."

Samantha glances out of her window. The atmosphere continues to be increasingly obscene. They appear to be traveling from a bad neighborhood to worse.

At least, this doesn't amaze me. Samantha assumed that she might be exposed to the nasty underbelly of society, especially after the electronics shop. Still, she holds onto the hope that it won't worsen. This is not something to be counted on, though.

"So," Samantha decides to continue the conversation regardless of the odd direction it appears to take. "What about before you woke up this morning?" Secretly, she wants to determine whether he's a robot or a cyborg.

"Don't know, don't care." He responds without averting his attention from the road.

"You don't?"

"If it doesn't help me complete my objective," Johnny Vinz clarifies, "I don't see the point in thinking about it."He may be a company man, after all. Though, hired guns have that same mentality. She would know because she has seen them up close several times. *Company man hired gun; either way, he doesn't seem to be a robot; he's a cyborg then.*

"I would like to know where I came from." She says matter-of-factly as she can muster.

"Well, you're organic."

That was rude. "That's the second time you people have referred to me as an organic." *One terse statement for another.*

Vinz chuckles. "You people?" He says between his laughter.

"Yeah, you robotics."

"That's the best title you could come up with, robotic?" Vinz laughs again.

Samantha finds herself more insulted that he is not than she was at the pejorative language that he and Christian Drake use to describe people like her.

"You have your names for us," she snorts, "and we have our names for you." Samantha Shaw's voice contorts with the slightest twang of sass. "But honestly, is it a problem that I don't believe in augmenting my body with computer chips and circuitry?"

"Not a problem." Johnny Vinz explains. "But you'll never understand what it's like to have access to all this information. It's too much to deal with on a constant flow, let alone all the backlogs."

What does that have to do with anything? "So, what you're saying is: you have too much on your mind to worry about little things like who you are? What happened yesterday? Whether you're human or just some computer program?" Samantha is inadvertently ridiculing him. But she's not sorry about it. *He's crude.* She thinks to herself. *He deserves ridicule.*

"Exactly."

Samantha feels anger unconsciously and tightens her back and chest muscles. *This man is more infuriating than that psychotic Colonel or the manipulative detective. And he's not trying to destroy my entire life. He's just an ass.*

"You're missing out." Samantha jokes, trying to break the tension in the car and her body.

"Yesterday was awesome."

They both share a laugh at her little joke.

The car stops at its destination. *How long have they been driving?* Samantha wonders as they exit the vehicle. It's daytime. And not early morning. It appears to be mid-afternoon. The sky illuminates under the powerful glow of the sun.

Samantha stares at their objective. A large apartment building that once housed Zayyir.

Now, it is a safe haven for the lowest of Chamariko's population.

In previous cultures, this type of building would be called a project; more than that, it would be condemned and marked as unsafe for anyone to dwell in. But the term 'project' is outlawed. Moreover, they restricted quite a few words. As if prohibiting a statement made the truth of its definition obsolete.

Zayyir may have only been nine years old when the security forces took him into custody, but he'd already been labeled the most dangerous hacker in all of Chamariko.

If this virus turns out to be working by his hand, Samantha Shaw thinks as she stares at the thirty-story building, *then he was even more incredible than all the corporations realized.* Which would be odd because they typically do not miss talent.

Held together by magnetic bonding agents, the building is in incredible disrepair. Samantha notices the makeshift remedies that keep the building from collapsing.

Low-tech innovations like home-made cement fill fractures at the building's foundation. Broken windows are sealed with hardened jell constructed from household cleaning supplies.

Clearly, nothing about this building is up to the standards that Samantha has become accustomed to seeing. Whoever patched this building together did not work on the corporate dime. Each aspect of the building's maintenance would only pass inspection in the 'corporate cul-de-sac'.

"Well, this is lovely," Samantha remarks, staring at the decrepit building. "So, what do we do?"

"You are going to wait here." He answers as he prepares to exit the company vehicle.

"What?"

Vinz flashes her an honest glance. "Look," he begins, "I can move around that place because I see everything."

"You're going to sneak into an apartment building in broad daylight? Let's wait till night." Johnny Vinz shakes his head. "I can avoid everything; I just can't be worrying about you as well in the process."

"Everything?" Samantha didn't mean to sound so snarky.

"I have access to every schematic that has ever been logged on or off the network, and I am capable of seeing in every known spectrum of light. But every citizen there will think we're after them or, at the very least, they will see corporate sector members on their turf."

Samantha acknowledges his reasoning with a nod. *Cops and criminals don't typically get along.* "So, if we're detected," she responds, "we start a panic?"

"We start a riot." Johnny Vinz corrects. "Advancement Industries does not do business here for a reason." When corporate governance was established, much blood was shed during the 'age of consolidation'. But, unfortunately, the war for authority and legitimacy never ended for many of the downtrodden."

"Then how did they catch Zayyir in the first place?" The words escape Samantha's mouth before she realizes she's talking. Vinz doesn't say anything; he simply eyes her with a cold stare, or at least she thinks he does. One can never tell with him wearing those opaque shields over his eyes. "Sorry." Even if she wasn't wrong, this is not the time for a political conversation about the United Corporations' ruthless tactics in establishing dominance over Chamariko.

"Contact Drake and fill him in, twiddle your thumbs, stare at the sky, and imagine pretty, pretty butterflies. I don't care what you do; just stay in the car." And with that, Johnny Vinz gets out of the car and starts toward the rundown domicile. He stealthily maneuvers into a hidden entrance of the apartment building, expertly avoiding cameras and prying eyes. Once inside the building, Johnny Vinz hides in the nooks and crannies of the apartment hallways. He avoids criminal and civilian elements who migrate through the building's interior as they conduct tedious tasks in their mundane lives.

As he passes various apartments in the building, Johnny Vinz hears the sounds of mischievous dealings as shady business dealings are conducted behind many of the doors that he passes. Interestingly, these low-class criminals are similar to the social elite in the 'corporate cul-de-sac'.

Though Johnny Vinz hides in the blind spots that riddle the building, he walks like a man without a care in the world. As if he were leisurely moving into an office building of his employment. Since he can see every object, nothing and no one can surprise him.

With immaculate precision, Johnny Vinz moves toward Zayyir's apartment. He reaches the hacker's domicile. He touches the doorknob with his pointer and middle finger. It is locked with corporate barriers. *Interesting,* he thinks to himself as he inspects the seals. Residents never touched the electronic walls. Even after a fifteen-year absence, Zayyir is still an enigma to them. A child that challenged the empire. They revere him, even in death.

The barriers appear to have a time stamp from when they were originally sealed. Johnny Vinz can do nothing but shake his head. Never touched in all the fifteen years of his departure from the living. No scavengers, looters, businessmen, no one who would disturb the sanctity of Zayyir's holy dwelling.

Symbols and writings fill the wall on either side of the entrance to the former hacker's apartment. Much of the script indicates the people's awe at the young prodigy's courage tocombat the evil corporation Advancement Industries. Markings depict Christian Drake as some spiteful entity raging against the child's altruistic exploits. And, of course, promises of Zayyir's return and his great intent and capability of righting the wrongs of Chamariko, returning the people to some Utopian society where technology no longer dictates the worth of any individual.

Johnny Vinz easily hacks the outdated locking system and steps casually into the apartment, unnoticed and without leaving a log of his presence on the antique time stamp.

He closes the door behind him and walks into the living room. Unbeknownst to him, this is the last place Zayyir, and his father were free people. Nothing is moved from the day when Zayyir warned his father of the imposing security forces sent by Christian Drake and Advancement Industries. Now covered in dust, the couch sits idly as if waiting for its owner to return. While dead, the television continues to anticipate activation to once again project images of newscasters reading the mangled truth and outright lies in their approved scripts.

The apartment is trashed as it had been left fifteen years ago. Curtains ever so slightly wave greetings to Johnny Vinz as a light breeze blows into the room from an open terrace window. From the disheveled nature of his apartment, both Zayyir and his father appeared to have been pack-rat.

Broken equipment dismantled electronics, and useless trinkets clutter every surface of the apartment.

Following a small unobstructed trail, Johnny Vinz moves from the living room into the bedroom.

Drapes block the sun's brilliant shine from invading the tiny room. Zayyir's computer appears to be broken beyond repair. Essential components are missing, and the home-made system lies dormant. It is one of the few personal effects disturbed since Zayyir and his father attempted their great escape.

And why wouldn't Advancement Industries excavate the child's incredible inventions? Any innovation that could be gleaned from the youthful hacker's technology would be of the highest priority.

Many of the machine's internal circuits are fried or frayed from the forced removal of the computer's guts. Even in its disrepair, however, it is an impressive machine.

Johnny Vinz inspects the advanced antique, moving various wires and components with his fingertips as he evaluates the home-made machine. Finally, enough of the computer remains operational for Vinz to rewire and activate it. He quickly goes to work on the dismantled equipment, finding alternative methods of re-activating the system. Luckily, the trinkets of technology that litter the floor come into use as he works to electronically reincarnate this discarded machine.

Strangely, this feels natural to him, not as if he were drawing on some internal program, but as if he were living some lost memory.

When power is restored, errors and warning signs appear on the screen.

"Yeah, yeah," Johnny Vinz says as he types exemptions into command lines from the keyboard. "Tell me something I don't know." Vinz hacks through the computer, searching for uncorrupted and readable files. "There's got to be something here that's even remotely usable." He whispers to himself as he continues his search.

A shadowy figure quietly stands behind Johnny Vinz behind his back and outside his awareness.

The computer boots up and runs a specific program. Next, Johnny Vinz sees an official emblem of Advancement Industries lights up on the screen, followed by a text indicating the location of an off-the-books testing facility.

Johnny notices a file named 'CTMS project'. The thoughts of Vinz are transposed into commands on the screen. It is a simple request: *What is the CTMS project?* A robotic voice speaks from Zayyir's speakers, reading the description of this odd project name. This project that Zayyir stumbled upon in his first journey into Skeleton filled internal documentation of Advancement industries. Johnny Vinz listens patiently as the summary is given.

"This document, attachment 11.2b, appears to describe a highly unethical and dangerous experiment conducted by Trans Production Inc. called the Cerebral Transudation and Modulation Synthesizer (CTMS). The CTMS is designed to interpret cognitive thought into readable programming, but the experiment resulted in a 100% fatality rate for all 23 subjects.

The document also mentions a waiver exonerating Trans Production Inc., likely the rival company of Advancement Industries, for any complications brought by the experiment. Additionally, there are notes on the personal experiences of Subject 23, including erratic cognitive movement, glitches, and an inability to decipher reality-based thoughts.

The cause of fatality is still undetermined, but data suggests CTMS malfunction. The subject/CTMS connection was made at 2:29:31 A.M., and the connection was lost at 2:29:33 A.M., resulting in the nervous system shutdown and death of the subject. The document notes that the cause of connection loss is still unknown.

Overall, this document reveals a highly unethical and dangerous experiment that resulted in the deaths of all subjects. The fact that a waiver exists suggests that those involved knew the experiment was illegal and potentially lethal. If this document were to be leaked, it would likely result in severe legal consequences for those involved and a public outcry against the company. It is important that such experiments never take place again and that proper regulations and ethical guidelines are in place to prevent such atrocities from occurring in the future.

It seems that Christian Drake's curiosity over Attachment 11.2b led him to discover the potential of the CTMS machine, which was eventually renamed the "Vinz Project". However, negotiations with John Demure were difficult as the two conglomerates had different ideas on how to evolve the experiment. The CTMS Project resulted from a year-long arbitration, combining the R&D departments of both conglomerates and placing Dark Facilities throughout the Urban Cities.

The CTMS Project's mission was to ensure the perpetual advancement of the Human Species, resulting in the creation of fifteen Dark Facilities.

John Demure headed an experimental campaign to perfect the CTMS technology, while Christian Drake was more interested in fusing a human nervous system with a synthetic one. The testing cost thousands of lives and trillions of dollars, resulting in a maddening stopping point called the "Nervous System Equation."

One of the scientists on the original project, Nicholas Young, was requested back into the project and was able to solve the "Nervous System Equation." However, he was never seen again after bringing resolution to this problem."

Johnny Vinz expands his connection to files in Advancement Industries. With the sanction of Christian Drake, he is able to track the timeline of the dark facilities mentioned in the file. Through a series of cross-references of timelines and locations, Vinz is able to deduce the facility that Zayyir had been taken to after his capture.

The thought crowds Johnny Vinz' mind as he commits the address to memory.

He notices a secure file that he easily hacks into. The screen goes dark before the text begins to rise from the bottom of the screen. These outdated systems always took their time booting files into the program.

The text reads:

SYSTEM ACTIVATED...
SCANNING...
ANALYZING...
CONNECTING...
SYNCING SYSTEM WITH SUBJECT...
INITIALIZING IN...
3...
2...
1...

Strange, indecipherable pictures, hidden behind a fuzzy haze, flash quickly on the screen. Each image, some horrific, some mundane, and some emotional, glimmer instantly and disappear in the blink of an eye.

Eerie sounds accompany the images. These sounds make no worldly sense. Instead, they are a hybrid of organic gurgles and electronic alerts spit out from the speakers on either side of the computer.

ADJUSTING...

The semblance of a voice is heard in the obscurity of sounds. Its words are indecipherable and cryptic.

ADJUSTING...

The images begin to slow and start coming into focus.

FINAL ADJUSTMENT...

Johnny Vinz sees everything.

13

Johnny Vinz is now in the virtual world of Zayyir's computer program. The system may be over a decade old, but he can still access it as he accessed the files in Christian Drake's mind.

He sees through the perspective of an unknown subject. The distorted images of his surroundings slowly come into focus. He is sitting in a restaurant; though he can deduce this from his immediate surroundings, much of the world beyond his elegantly dressed table is still completely out of focus.

A beautiful young woman sits across from him at the table. She lightly rubs her index finger on the rim of a half-filled wine glass. She wears a coy smile. Her ethnically attractive features are accented by her 'diamond in the rough' red dress and second-hand jewelry. She is clearly not among the social elite, but her attire explains that she is not part of the riffraff of the quarantine zone.

Since this is some kind of flashback, Johnny Vinz is still determining if the quarantine zone even exists in this time period. And since he is immersed in a computer program, Johnny Vinz considers whether this is a legitimate memory or a projected reality of some desired past.

His focus shifts from her to the rest of the restaurant. He does not control the movement of his gaze; instead, he is simply following the activity as an audience member in a movie theater. Nothing but fuzzy images can be seen, moving like waiters and patrons.

"So..." His vision returns to the girl. "Tell me about yourself."

As if her question broke his reality, the world distorts and shifts. Johnny Vinz no longer sees the girl. He is no longer in the restaurant. Instead, he feels the strong embrace of padded wrist restraints holding his arms to a gurney. Nothing can be seen but brilliant fluorescent light.

Again, his vision shivers as the world transitions to a new reality.

Johnny Vinz now sits on a couch, looking at the same girl who sits close to him, nestled in a pile of pillows. They are in some antique apartment. The incredible technological innovations that citizens of Chamariko have become accustomed to enjoying. Plaster walls with neutral colors sloppily painted offer little visual elegance; instead, the room seems to be a prison cell masquerading as an apartment.

She stares at him with tenderness in her eyes.

Johnny Vinz feels a hint of recognition as his uncontrollable focus remains steadfast, returning her gaze. *I remember this.* He thinks to himself as the two stare at each other.

He hears himself thinking the words, but it is not his voice. He must be experiencing the world through the body of someone else. Rather than focus on this odd discrepancy, his internal voice continues speaking to him; *I said something funny.* The indecipherable words are projected and exist only in the ether, like a voice-over. Johnny Vinz thinks he must be thinking thoughts but cannot determine what ideas he may be thinking.

Even though Johnny Vinz feels his mouth move, only the garbled sounds of a strange man's voice are heard.

The girl appears to understand the garbled gibberish from Johnny Vinz' lips.

"Whatever, shut up." She says while she laughs lovingly.

Again, the indiscernible chatter comes out of Johnny Vinz' disconnected body.

"I love you too." A bashful smile stretches across her face.

Johnny Vinz hears the strange language formed from his mouth one more time.

Silhouettes of several doctors are once again superimposed over the woman's vision and the prison-like atmosphere. That brilliant fluorescent light is back as well. They begin to overshadow the blissful scene.

"Maybe, we should go somewhere. Just you and me. What do you think?" She says as her image begins to fade away, disappearing as some forgotten dream.

The peaceful world containing her and the happy memory dissolves, and now the dazzling operating light of some hospital room is all that can be seen.

The silhouettes are doctors who surround the surgical table. Johnny Vinz sees this from the disembodied viewpoint of some unknown individual's experience.

"Doctor," a voice emits from one of the shadowy figures. Johnny Vinz can only assume that a nurse is speaking by the way she gives respectful subordination to the other shadows.

The figure appears to be staring down at him as she says. "His eyes are open again."

"Interesting." Another shadow responds. "Make a note." The human silhouette reaches down to the center of Johnny Vinz' sight and gently closes his eyes.

When his eyes open again, Johnny Vinz peers off the edge of a cliff into a vast blue sea. The ridge itself is a peaceful scene of grass and dandelions. The sound of distant crashing waves and singing seagulls fills the air with a blissful ambiance.

The girl, that same girl from the restaurant, that girl from the apartment, that unknown girl who seems to follow him in his dreams, stands at his side. This time, however, he recognizes her. The owner of his remembered fantasy knows her and does so intimately, as though they have loved each other for quite some time. Her name is Jessica. She is dressed in an elegant silk dress. The hem of her beautiful white garment flows majestically in the salty ocean breeze.

Johnny Vinz can't help but admire her exquisite dress with loving intent. Something about her feels warm and comforting. With her, he feels at peace.

"You were right about this place." She says, admiring the view as he admires her.

Johnny Vinz feels the urge to reach up to her, to touch her, and embrace her. But he can't. His hands are shackled. *Why are my hands shackled in this Utopian experience?*

"This view is beautiful." She admires it with a blissful smile. "It almost makes me wish I could stay out here forever."

It's true. Even as a disconnected observer, Johnny Vinz wishes he could stay on this beach with her. He wishes he wasn't some masterful design produced by Advancement Industries. He doesn't want to be a cybernetic monstrosity created by the corporate overlords. But he also cannot determine if these emotions flourish from a genuine desire to be with this woman that he only knows from a program deep in the bowels of Zayyir's computer or if they are something tangible that swells from his true self. He cannot decipher the truth of this. He cannot determine the origin of his feelings. He can only understand the outcome of their intoxicating desire. There is nothing he could want to do for now. He wishes this was not a computer simulation. He wishes this was his memory and not a simple observation that he stumbled across researching some horrifying virus that threatened Chamariko. He wishes he could be with her, here, forever.

But that is not possible. This beach does not exist. At least, not anymore. Johnny Vinz would venture to believe that scenery like this hasn't existed for quite some time.

"You can forget about everything." She continues, her eyes fixated on the horizon. "And the air. Just smell that ocean air." He can smell it. The light scent of salt touches his nose and captivates the senses with its salutary odor. Johnny Vinz inhales a deep breath through his nostrils, allowing himself to fully embrace his surroundings.

As he does, he stares at the brilliant yellow sun that peers lovingly down on the world. Then, it transforms into that cold fluorescent light of some unknown operating table. An incredible pain shoots through his body. He wasn't inhaling to smell the serene scent of a perfect moment. Instead, he was gulping air to scream in terrible agony.

"So..." Her voice pulls him back into her world. The place he wishes that he could stay. By this point, Johnny Vinz wants to disregard any mission he may have had and live in this fantasy with Jessica. In this false reality, he exhales peacefully. His body is free of the torturous silhouettes. "Tell me about yourself."

There's a distortion, not of the memory, but by a mechanical error. Even lost in this virtual utopia, Johnny Vinz can feel his body shiver. Some corrupted file interrupts his memory. The glitch causes a disruption in his thoughts and breaks his intoxicated feelings for the woman. It is a feeling of ripping love from the depths of his heart. It feels like death. Or at least the residual sensation makes him yearn for it. That pain of losing something pure. Natural emotions that were felt initially by Adam and Eve in their tragic fall from grace.

What's wrong? Johnny Vinz wonders as he corrects the error. *Did Jessica notice the error as well?*

They are back in the apartment. The transitions could be more accessible for Johnny Vinz to keep up with. None of the memories are connected with one another.

Jessica stands in a confrontational posture. Behind her, Johnny Vinz can see himself in a mirror. Or at least, he believes it's himself. The mirror shows fragments of the face. It is the face of the owner of these memories. The one who lived this life. The one who lost this life a long time ago. There are no distinguishing features. It's like the glass is broken into fragmented pieces. But it's not. The mirror is not broken; his reflection is.

"How will we ever get out of this place if you can't even hold a job?"

Johnny Vinz feels a rush of defensive feelings. "So," he feels himself protesting, "this is my fault, now?"

"Seven jobs in three years. Who should I blame?"

"It's not like there are a lot of opportunities for a former felon." Finally, Vinz has some clue as to who this individual is. Still, more information is needed to track him down. Something about this moment reignites his desire to solve the puzzle that brought him here.

"It's been years!" Jessica screams. "How long are you going to use that as a crutch?"

"You wanted me to go straight. That's what I'm trying to do." This subject has lived outside the confines of polite society. A mobster? An extremist?

The woman touches her belly. It's that kind of touch. One that only a woman can make and only at a specific time. *She is pregnant.*

"That's not good enough anymore!" Jessica cries out, tears preparing to escape from her eyes and streak down her beautiful face. It hurts him, even if this is not his memory, to see her in such pain. "If you would just try a little harder."

Vinz feels the fire of frustration burning. "What do you want from me!? I've given you everything I can! What are you missing?"

"What am I missing?" Jessica responds in shock. "Look around you." She opens her arms and turns her head to draw his attention to the menial apartment. "LOOK!!"

Johnny Vinz is jolted back into the operating room. Piercing pain pulses through his body as if it were carried by his blood. He can feel his face twisting in a fit of pain and terror. Johnny Vinz, who is the subject, tries desperately to see everything in the room with little success.

His head is restrained. Electrodes are attached all over his shaven skull.

The doctor peers down at him. There is an air of annoyance in his glare. "Will someone tape those eyes closed, please?"

14

Samantha waits in the car. A screen in the dashboard portrays the video image of Christian Drake. He is a vibrant-looking man sitting in front of huge windows that peer out with a view of the entire city of Chamariko.

Although the brilliant sun stands high in the sky as it explains to the people of Chamariko that midday has been reached, the battle for supremacy between nature's stars and man's lights continues their continual assault on each other in the virtual windows of Christian Drake's fake office.

Any signs of his illness are hidden by filters. Those incredible tricks of visual media work marvelously to deceive even the harshest scrutiny of the most detailed observers into believing that Christian Drake is a powerful man at the peak of his physical prowess.

Samantha tries not to show her disbelief in his presentation. Having seen the truth of his degraded body, she is not swayed by this authentic deep fake.

This must be the synthetic appearance that he uses for his meetings. Samantha Shaw thinks to herself. T*he correct* *physical version of Christian Drake is sickly and broken by his disease. Much more than what I'm looking at on this screen.* The false rendition of Christian Drake is so believable that if Samantha had not just met the man, she would have fallen for this electronic facade like everyone else.

"So, there's nothing out of the ordinary?" Christian Drake asks through the video.

Samantha shakes her head. "Nothing that I can tell. But there's so much about him that I don't understand." Samantha is not used to working with so little information. Her career consists of being presented with an overabundance of information and having to sift through it all to find the needles that hide in the mountainous stack. This is the first time she has been asked to directly assess a subject. And to suddenly be instructed to evaluate the brainchild of Advancement Industries. Samantha Shaw may have been intimidated to meet the chief executive officer of Advancement Industries, but now she's being asked to criticize the effectiveness of his work. He truly is not a man who acts with prideful intent.

"That's fine." Christian Drake concedes, "as long as he isn't showing symptoms of infection."

"I don't mean to question your judgment, but why did you assign me to this investigation in the first place?" She can't contain herself. Samantha needs at least one puzzle to be solved for her. Up to this point, she's felt like a shipwrecked survivor floating aimlessly at sea.

"Because you're organic." Christian Drake responds.

Is this a dig? Or an answer to my question? Samantha feels a little insulted by his simple reply. "Everyone keeps mentioning that." She begins, shaking her head with a disgruntled frown. "What is that supposed to mean?"

She is aware of the stigma surrounding those who never augmented their bodies. Social elites see them as cowards who forgo the most basic advancements that society can offer. As a result, many in the upper echelon of the corporate technocracy have called organics the Neanderthals of Chamariko. With little social authority to resist such bigotry, most organics consciously embrace the vocabulary, even wielding it as a weapon against the smiths of its terminology.

Samantha has endured passive and direct ridicule from her peers and supervisors. It is something that she's become accustomed to experiencing. Rather than engage in some political battle that appeared to continue into eternity, Ms. Shaw sought to let her work make any retaliation for her. Nothing could be more gratifying than outworking the augmented as an organic.

But to be selected for some world-saving assignment and denigrated simultaneously is a unique bite at her pride. Nevertheless, such an opportunity will do wonders for her career. And when she passes by those augmented sycophants in the towers of corporate power, Samantha Shaw will have no problem looking down at those who once looked down on her.

Christian Drake nods with an expression of acknowledgment of her frustration. He may be the most powerful man in Chamariko, perhaps even the world, but he is still human. This king of Babylon, whose authority knows no bounds understands more than most about the incredible shame one can feel when seen as fragile by the rest of the world. He has spent most of his life hiding the perceived weakness of his body. So why would he judge her for hers?

"This virus," Drake begins, "or whatever it turns out to be, only affects machines and mechanical designs. If someone has an arm augmentation, the virus attacks that arm. Someone else has a brain augmentation; then the virus attacks their brain." Samantha Shaw suddenly realizes her most significant asset and why she was selected for such an important assignment.

"I'm immune?" Her mouth swings open, and her hair is neatly tucked behind her ear. Christian Drake nods. He flashes a look of compassion. The corporate genius purses his lips and lightly shifts them to one side. The eyes of this great man soften as though he were trying to silently express to her one crucial message: 'This is why I need you'.

His benevolent countenance proves to Samantha Shaw that she is talking to a computer-enhanced image and not the authentic CEO of Advancement Industries. Christian Drake, chairman of the most powerful corporation in Chamariko, cannot move anything beyond his eyes. Let alone showing such a sincere sign of compassion and vulnerability.

Samantha suddenly realizes the importance of Johnny Vinz and the success of his mission. Johnny Vinz is not just the brainchild of Advancement Industries. He is the hope of Christian Drake. Yet, with all his power, he is powerless. Nothing will stop his debilitating disease. There is no cure. And even if there was, there is no cure for death. Time brings age, and age brings death. Christian Drake made Johnny Vinz disprove a quiet truth that all men know.

This disease that Christian Drake suffers from, one that has tormented mankind long before the 'age of consolidation', long before the erection of Chamariko, is proof of man's inability to control his destiny. With all the advancements humanity has made, they still cannot free themselves from the debilitating end that is brought with age. Mankind is still nothing more than a plaything to nature. Nothing changes that. Not medicines or augmentation. Nothing. In the end, man is still just that, man.

"Please, inform me if you see any irrational behavior from Johnny Vinz."

"Yes, of course I will."

The image of Christian Drake cuts out and leaves Samantha in the car, staring at a blank screen. The last vestiges of Christian Drake and his incredible office view dissolve into darkness. Samantha leans back in her chair and exhales slowly. Her body sinks into the fabricated leather as she releases tension. She now considers the small trickle of information to be a good thing. This one revelation is enough to liquefy her mind.

This was my actual assignment the whole time. Ms. Shaw thinks as she stares aimlessly down the downtrodden street. *I'm not here to find the source of a virus. My job is monitoring Johnny Vinz. I can't get infected by this computer virus, but he is still vulnerable, no matter how advanced he may seem.*

Samantha's attention rises to the apartment building. But she seems to see it differently with this new revelation. Her eyes lock on the hidden entrance where Johnny Vinz disappeared in search of clues to the origins of this ferocious Mayhem Virus.

In the front of the building, near the entrance, Samantha notices a shrine dedicated to Zayyir. Flowers in varying states of decay litter a small section around an awning that lifts up into a slight arch. Pictures and candles recently placed are nestled in small gaps between the dying foliage.

I wish I had known this earlier. Samantha thinks. *What am I looking for? Has he already shown symptoms?* Samantha works to actively recall her experience with this incredible technological innovation. She is no longer concerned with whether Johnny Vinz is a cyborg or a robot. She is simply concerned with whether he has already been infected by this perilous virus and if he poses a danger to her. He would be the most terrifying zombie Chamariko could fathom if infected. He would also be the most terrifying proof in history. He would be proof that humanity lost to the virus.

15

The strange figure, standing beyond the awareness of Johnny Vinz, moves closer to the innovation of Advancement Industries. He stares in a trance at the computer screen, his mind tethered intimately to the program, unaware of its presence.

He is physically vulnerable in moments like these, uniquely attached to the virtual world.

Though eerie, the figure does not appear to be malicious. Instead, it idly moves closer as if waiting for Johnny Vinz to complete his work in the machine.

Johnny sees odd images flash across his view inside the computerized reality as he mentally re-calibrates the program to the next set of memories.

The world re-configures, and Johnny Vinz finds himself in a new place. Jessica has yet to follow him to this memory. Her absence is noticed by a sinking feeling in his heart.

This time, when the memory details come to fruition, he sits in the driver's side of some antique vehicle; at least, it is antique by the modern standards of Chamariko.

Johnny Vinz wanders, even lost in the intimate nature of his memory, if these events occurred before Zayyir walked the earth or if he is, in fact, seeing through the eyes of Zayyir himself. *This can't be Zayyir's memory.* He thinks, trying to shield himself from false perceptions of this reality. *Zayyir never lived past 10 years of age.*

Even though Jessica is not with him, Johnny Vinz is not alone. Someone sits on the passenger side of the vehicle. Internally, Johnny Vinz recognizes this individual. There is a long connection between the two. *These were childhood friends.*

The friend, this nameless individual whose name is incapable of being rendered in Johnny Vinz' recollection, glances at him with a concerned expression.

"Are you sure you want to do this?" The friend asks, holding some ancient weapon in his hands.

Johnny Vinz feels himself turn his attention as the subject's memory demands an awareness of the weapons collected in the backseat. He grabs one of the deadly tools and checks the chamber to ensure a projectile is readied in the steel pipe.

"I need money." Johnny Vinz feels the words blurt from the subject's mouth before he knows it. "Once we do this," he continues, "I'm done."

"I heard that before." The friend laughs unconsciously and shakes his head. "This time, it's for real." Johnny Vinz knows the truth behind the subject's statement. Remembering the moments with Jessica has made him keenly aware of this subject's need for monetary stability. He needs money, not for himself, but for his child. And he needs to leave the criminal underbelly of Chamariko for the same reason.

He's a criminal. Johnny Vinz thinks as he watches the events continue to play out. *This can't be Zayyir. He was not this kind of criminal. His weapons were keyboards and monitors, not guns and bullets.*

The friend nods with a sigh. "Alright." Weapons are locked and loaded. Masks are pulled over to hide their identities. "Let's do this."

Everything in this virtual world fades away. For a moment, Johnny Vinz believes that he may be dealing with another error in the code, some corrupted file that works to inhibit his ability to observe the rest of the historical memory. But his blank vision only looms for a moment before returning to the same memory of the car as if some jump cut bounced him forward in time. Though Johnny Vinz cannot be sure what transpired, what he sees is evidence enough of the situation.

The friend jumps back into the passenger side, breathing heavily. They must have been running for some time. The subject's vision, which is Johnny Vinz' vision, is blurry from fatigue and excitement. Something is significantly different about the friend. He has lost what relaxed demeanor he might have had previously and is now covered in blood. In addition, the sticky liquid is beginning to show signs of drying.

"What was that!?" He exclaims.

The subject glances down at his lap. Johnny Vinz can feel the rush of fear storming through his veins as if he were the subject in this very moment, lost and scared with the discovery that he is overwhelmed in a situation far beyond his control. Blood also covers his torso and legs. His hands are saturated by the red liquid. It's not his. There is not a wound on his body. But Johnny Vinz knows that seeing this much-liquefied flesh means someone's life has been taken.

"I had to do something." Johnny Vinz, who is the subject in Zayyir's computer program, protests defensively, "he went for his piece."

"You're getting blood all over my car!"

Johnny can feel the tension between both the subject and his friend.

"We need to ditch this car." The friend thinks aloud.

What happened? This internal voice is separated from Johnny Vinz. But still, he wishes he knew.

"What?" The subject of Johnny's vision asks. "Where should we go?"

Johnny Vinz can hear the subject's thoughts. *What have I done?* He may be disconnected from this individual by time and place, but he still feels a strange connection to whoever it is.

It must be the girl. Johnny Vinz thinks to himself as events in this virtual memory continue to progress. His strange emotional attachment to Jessica is the only link.

Something in the program must have embedded a fervent desire into the viewer. This type of technology may be more common practice in modern Chamariko, but Zayyir was indeed a genius in understanding how to implement it when he was alive.

The subject looks at his friend. There is so much fear in his trembling gaze. His hands won't stop shaking.

"What are we going to do?"

The subject, and Johnny Vinz, need answers, but his friend doesn't seem to have them.

"I don't know! I just... I don't know."

They are on an empty, isolated highway. Hidden from society and help alike.

They have time to think, but it won't do them any good. They've crossed a line. Committed an action that cannot be undone.

The scene fades away once more. Again, initially confusing, but Johnny Vinz is becoming aware of the transitions. It is like moving locations in a movie; he is beginning to understand the overarching theme.

Johnny Vinz no longer sees the car or his friend. He is now in a cold dark place devoid of compassion. This place results from his desire to provide for his family. It is a place of steel and concrete.

Sitting in a prison cell Johnny Vinz, who sees from the subject's perspective, views the hopelessness of his situation. Etched markings catalog the lost time of previous prisoners.

A businessman stands outside the cell, wearing a 'million-dollar suit'. He stares at the subject with shark eyes. They peer at him through the steel bars lacking any kind of compassion.

Chamariko has always been full of individuals such as this. Emotionless individuals are only concerned with the accomplishment of their objectives. The city never needed robotic servants with people like this walking around.

"This is the third strike. They are going to kill you, my friend." This heartless businessman is clearly not a friend, but, unfortunately, he is the only lifeline that the subject has left.

Johnny Vinz can feel himself wishing events would not continue. So they didn't have to play out in the way that he already knows that they will. But he is a passive observer. An audience member with no authority over these events and how they transpire because they have already transpired. This is not a moment to take action; it is a time to see what measures have been taken.

At this point, two memories begin superimposing over each other. Johnny Vinz is in this prison but also in that lovely apartment like some apparition. Not to be seen or felt by any of its occupants.

Distorted images of that essential woman, Jessica, fade over his vision as if his mind were splitting the focus between these two events. Because of this, she does not appear as the solid image Johnny Vinz has become accustomed to in his visions; instead, Jessica is a translucent woman somberly sitting with a newborn baby in her arms.

She stares blankly into nothing as if peering into the void of her own soul. The scene gently hazes over the imagery of the cell.

Friends and family surround her. Celebrating or consoling, it is unclear. A banner hangs on the wall just above the couch. It was the couch where they shared such intimate moments. The same couch that witnessed their terrible fight over finances led him to his irreversible mistake. And now, it is the couch that very same supports her in her time of tragedy. The banner reads in bold letters: “WELCOME HOME”.

“The death penalty for you, my friend.” Words from this drone of business re-centers Johnny Vinz’ attention on the stony prison cell. “Leaving a wife and a newly born son, from what I hear.” The businessman continues.

It is a dirty tactic, attacking the loss of a man’s family. But one that Advancement Industries built many of their negotiations on.

The distorted image of the woman, his woman, sustains over the dark prison cell. Some of the party-goers slowly fade away, vanishing into obscurity.

“You can appeal,” he continues, “but I think we know what’s going to happen with that.” A slight nod of acknowledgment, but it’s clear that the businessman is not trying to offer hope.

The worlds of this prison and his apartment shutters as if distorted by another glitch in the programming.

"Who are you?" The subject asks.

"A man who can help." The businessman disappears from his position and reappears inside the cell with the subject, moving like some ghostly phantom on its way to possessing an unsuspecting victim.

"You know what I have here?" The cold businessman with shark's eyes holds a folder filled with documents in his hand. "This is your last chance."

More of the party-goers evaporate from the party. The apartment is becoming as empty and uninviting as this prison cell. But Jessica still stares absentmindedly at an emptiness that once held her heart.

"A get out of jail free card." Continues this high-class individual. Johnny Vinz can only assume that he is an executive from Advancement Industries. But he needs to find out if that corporation exists in the timeline of this memory. "I want you to be part of something important."

Only a few guests remain. Jessica is nearly as alone in the apartment as she feels in her heart.

"And once it's over, you can see your family again." He holds up the contract. "All you have to do is sign this."

The woman now sits alone on the apartment couch, clutching her child.

Dissolving once again from his place in the prison cell, the businessman with shark's eyes appears even closer to the subject. Now, he is standing over his distraught target in an imposing fashion. He waves a pen in the subject's face and holds the contract up.

"Sign it." He demands in a passive voice.

What is that? The subject's interior monologue questions. It is not a thought from Johnny Vinz, nor one that could be found in the program's code. Instead, it is as if the subject were reaching from the ethereal plain to echo their ancient thoughts.

A single word 'error' pulses over the image of Johnny Vinz' vision.

Johnny Vinz feels it again. *There is corruption in the data. This little excursion has nearly reached its conclusion.*

"You don't have a choice." The emotionless businessman continues. "You have to sign it. It's either this or death."

Everything dissolves away, leaving only a black void in its place.

"...Sign it."

In my mind?

A scrambled image and piercing screeching suddenly flood Johnny Vinz' awareness. The words' fatal error' flash gaudily in his vision, over and over again.

Once again, Johnny Vinz loses his vision, and the world is painted black. Only the steady hum of a flat line can be heard.

The bold, white words' connection lost' fill his blacked-out vision.

16

Johnny Vinz sighs as he takes a moment to collect himself. *An interesting story.* He thinks. *But nothing that brings me closer to Zayyir.* However, Johnny Vinz can't help but wonder why a young hacker like Zayyir would have such an elaborate program on his computer. Was the child researching the sins of Chamariko?

He notices another file hidden in the computer. It simply reads: "CTMA."

It may be some rogue industry that Zayyir was associated with. Johnny Vinz wonders. *Only one way to find out.* He wipes salty moisture from his face, prepares himself, and re-enters the digital world.

Johnny Vinz is no longer in the cell, the apartment, or the car; he finds himself in a dark void where he was in the previous program. In fact, he is far from the experience of the subject.

He is now peering into Christian Drake's office. It may not be as sophisticated as it was when he visited earlier. The technology is less sleek and advanced than

Johnny Vinz remembers, but there are enough similarities for Johnny Vinz to make the connection.

The scene is seen from security cameras and monitors mounted throughout the office.

Another difference and this is a big one, is that there are people in Christian Drake's office. So, at this point in time being shown, he is not reclusively hiding his corrosive disease from the public. In fact, Christian Drake does not show any of the significant signs of his genetic disability yet.

Johnny Vinz checks the timestamp deep in the program's language to get his bearings. This is some time in the past. Thirty years, perhaps.

Though younger, Christian Drake is still one of the older members in the room. He sits quietly with his eyes trained on the projector screen. Nothing is playing, but his eyes are still intently focused on the company emblem. His deep contemplation does not affect the other executives in the room, who are keenly aware of his presence and seek, in their own way, to illustrate their importance to the leader of Advancement Industries.

Sunbeams through the large windows of the office. These are genuine windows, not the holographic material Christian Drake usually used to fool the world.

A group of scientists, businessmen, and executives sit around a large, rectangular table. They watch the events of the subject's memory on a monitor.

Standing beside the screen, a youthful entrepreneur turns the display off. He faces the decision makers of Advancement Industries and prepares to continue his presentation.

Christian Drake appears youthful. The debilitating symptoms of his disease have not presented themselves.

"You've just seen the CTMA's first successful test with the help of subject 5. With the CTMA machine, 'CTMA' standing for Cerebral Transudation Modulation and Amplification, we successfully viewed the internal thoughts of subjects connected to the machine."

"How many subjects were involved in this experiment?" A young female executive who sits near the center of the table asks.

"Twenty-three."

She continues with her questioning, casually doodling as she speaks. "And how many survived?"

"One. The twenty-third subject survived disconnection from the machine, though there was permanent neurological damage." He pauses briefly, drinking a glass of water before continuing. "Subject twenty-three suffered a Cerebral Vascular Attack halfway through the experiment. Before we could clear the clot, the subject had a Grand-Male-Seizure. With further testing, we can decrease the risk."

"Meaning?" The female executive doesn't care one way or the other, but the record needs to reflect that she asked.

"He's brain dead, ma'am."

Another executive, sitting closer to Christian Drake in the arranged hierarchy, finishes scribbling in his notebook and begins speaking. "This particular experiment dealt specifically with reading thoughts. Is that correct?"

"Yes. But this machine should be capable of so much more in a short time."

"Like?" The male executive asks.

"In phase two," the youthful salesperson begins, "we will guide the subject's experiences by implanting specific thoughts in their minds."

"I'm not sure I understand that." The female executive interjects, no longer doodling on her paper and giving full attention to the young salesperson.

"Well," the salesperson begins, "to put it into layman's terms, just imagine being able to implant the idea of purple into someone's mind, seeing the ripple effect of conscious and subconscious thought. With this ability, we could begin dictating thoughts and actions by our subjects in future project phases. Does that answer your question?"

"Yes, thank you. Please continue." The female executive says as she leans back in her cushioned chair in contemplation.

"Once we've successfully implanted concepts and ideas, well, this machine will offer a variety of applications. Such as direct marketing and advertising, propaganda campaigns, social and military cohesion, and many other applications that could only be dreamed of without this technology."

The entrepreneur is being as candid as he can. He knows executives like the ones filling Christian Drake's office prefer to avoid fishing for information. But, if he's going to get his grant from Advancement Industries and embolden his modest company, he must be forthright.

"There is a note here about the subject's eyes. What is the significance of their eyes?" The female executive draws attention to the CTMA's documentation as she reclaims her command of the conversation. Each of the executives tries to illustrate their significance to Christian Drake. They are like newborn puppies suckling at their mother's teat, but in this litter, the runt does not die; they are demoted, which is much worse.

They fight for his attention like children vying for the position of favorite. And for good reason. Christian Drake's opinion of them dictates their role in the corporation.

"Yes." The entrepreneur answers. "We discovered that the CTMA machine didn't work properly when the subject was aware of their surroundings. The subject's eyes had to be closed for the machine to work properly."

"How long will it take to finish phase one?" She asks.

"We hope to be done with experimentation within a year."

"How long will phase two take to complete?" The male executive chimes in before his female counterpart can continue her questioning.

"Once phase one is completed, the following four phases should be concluded relatively quickly."

"How quickly?"

The entrepreneur can't help but smirk. These are the questions that he wished to hear. These questions mean he is on his way to being granted the money.

"Approximately two years per phase." He responds as directly as he can.

"Any chance of overlapping the experiments?"

The question breeds silence. It is so quiet that the low hum of air conditioning can be heard.

The entrepreneur was not ready for this question, but Christian Drake shows his intrigue and desire for a proper response to the answer by diverting his trance-like attention from the screen to the entrepreneur. The well-dressed, youthful man stands like a deer caught in headlights. His greatest fear is overselling his company's ability. Failing Advancement Industries could bankrupt an industry.

Finally, he can break through his nervous paralysis. "Yes. We could theoretically begin phase two now. Though we might have similar neurological difficulties as those in phase one."

"But those will be resolved within the year?" The executive, leaning casually back in his chair with the report in his hands, clearly doesn't care about the test subjects' loss of life or mental faculties. And why would he? This is about his career, not their lives.

"Each phase will develop its own additional complications. But, theoretically, yes."

Silence once again falls on the room. Finally, the executives are done asking their questions. Now, it is only for Christian Drake to make the final decision. He tries to stand in a dominating posture, but the trembling in his arms and shoulders shows clear signs of ALS. These were the final days before Christian Drake fell into seclusion, hiding his physical degradation in his private penthouse.

Drake gazes over his sycophantic followers and makes his decision.

"Phase two approved. Begin testing immediately. That is all."

17

Johnny Vinz jolts out of the computer program into reality. His eyes stay trained on the blank screen. The gaudy words 'Connection Lost' continue to fill the monitor.

Still standing in the modest apartment bedroom that once acted as a home for Zayyir and his father, Johnny Vinz continues, unaware of the strange entity hovering in the shadows behind him. This ethereal creature, staring at Johnny Vinz from its faceless facade, gently reaches a hand out and lightly touches his arm. As this essence makes contact with Johnny Vinz, a face emerges from the shadows, and the creature asks a single question.

"Who are you?" Zayyir whispers inquisitively.

The tender touch activates a sudden rash of movements in Johnny Vinz. He lifts up, spins, and reaches for the shadow in one motion. Just as he turns, the shadow disappears into the living room. Johnny Vinz rushes after Zayyir as the shadowy figure leaps over a couch in the center of the living room; the strange apparition heads for the front door.

In his intense pursuit, following closely behind Zayyir, Johnny Vinz quickly surges over the couch with incredible speed.

Suddenly, the illusion of his surroundings strips away, and Johnny Vinz discovers that he is not leaping toward the front door as he pursues Zayyir's phantom, but, in fact, he is not jumping over a couch at all. Instead, as the falsehood strips away, Johnny Vinz feels the cold iron of the makeshift fire escape that Zayyir's father had built so long ago. Far below, the hardened concrete comes into view nearly thirteen stories below.

Johnny Vinz has not been running after Zayyir; instead, he is running toward his death. With this sudden horrific realization, he feels a jolt of tightening muscles throughout his body.

His hand instinctively latches onto the cold iron railing and halts his fall with a vicious jerk. Dangling from the thirteenth story of the decrepit apartment building, Johnny Vinz quickly hauls himself back over the rusted railing into the safe confines of the living room. His heart pounds so powerfully in his chest that he can hear it rushing blood throughout his body.

On the empty street, standing just outside the company car, Samantha helplessly stares up at the terrifying events with no ability to influence them. Not even she knows what caused her to bring her attention to his situation, but she did.

Johnny Vinz lies on the floor, staring past the open window at the now ominous balcony railing.

"What the hell?" He exasperates aloud between gasping breaths.

Samantha continues fearfully watching his near-fatal accident from the safe confines of the city streets. Her face is contorted in shock and, strangely enough, a little embarrassment.

Moments after explaining to Christian Drake that Johnny Vinz was not exhibiting any irrational behavior she'd noticed in Captain Richards, he jumps out of a window.

It feels like an eternity to her before Johnny Vinz retreats down the thirteen stories of the broken-down apartment building and returns to the car. He acts as if nothing just happened. But it did.

Samantha stands in silence as Johnny Vinz moves toward the driver's side door of their company car as she searches for the right way to question him about his current state of mind.

"How did it go?" She finally questions in a meek voice as they re-enter the vehicle.

"There's an abandoned technology center hidden a couple dozen miles outside the city. It's a dark facility, so I couldn't connect it with Zayyir before. However, I discovered some information about it in the files on his computer." The car gently pushes forward as they start moving toward their next destination.

Samantha can only shake her head. *For some incredible technological advancement,* she thinks, *he sure does act like any normal human being when trying to avoid difficult questions.*

"So," Samantha continues investigating as they drive to their next destination. "Are we not going to talk about what just happened?"

"Nothing happened."

Is he in denial or infected? Samantha is fearfully trying to determine which would be more terrifying.

"You jumped out of a window." She blurts out uncontrollably as she harshly tucks stray strands behind her ear.

Johnny Vinz appears irked, which is frustrating for Samantha as it seems like a completely acceptable line of questioning for someone like him. Someone who just JUMPED OUT OF A WINDOW! His actions, nor his response to those actions, do not appear to be those of a sane person.

"I was chasing someone." He responds in a monotone voice.

"Out of a window?" She blurts uncontrollably again.

"Are you my doctor?" Vinz responds defensively, staring her in the eyes.

Samantha hesitates. "I just need to make sure you're not coming down with the same virus Captain Richards came down with. That didn't play out so well for anyone involved."

"I'm not."

He seems so sure. Samantha lightly shakes her head. *But so was Captain Richards.*

"How do you know?"

"I didn't black out, my vitals are still fluctuating sporadically, and I'm not mumbling crazy non-sequiturs. I know why I jumped out of the window... sort of. We'll deal with it later."

His speech is accelerated. Samantha decides to leave the conversation there. Whether he is infected or not, Johnny Vinz is dangerous to sit beside.

Samantha eyes him cautiously for a moment before returning her gaze outside the company vehicle. *He seems to have an answer for everything,* she thinks. *And I don't want to excite him into some kind of rage by challenging him.*

Any further questioning risks exposing her true motives. Even if Samantha Shaw believes this masterful design of Advancement Industries may still know her true ambition. He's been ahead of her this whole time.

The atmosphere changes once again. This time, Samantha sees the rural neighborhood primarily occupied by organics. She feels a nostalgic wave soothe her into her seat. This is a place she knows.

"I grew up in places like this," Samantha says sentimentally. "My parents raised me on a farm just like this on the other side of Chamariko."

She doesn't know why she shares her history with this emotionless cyborg. If Advancement Industries didn't care about her innocent childhood, then why would their creation? But, on the other hand, it may be a subconscious way for her to entice him into opening up. Regardless, she doesn't resist expressing her past in this car.

"My father was a governmentalist at heart. Truly believed in the guiding doctrine of state and senate." Samantha continues watching the rural countryside pass by as she thinks for a moment.

Advancement Industries and the entire corporate structure prefer to pretend that quaint homesteads still exist in places like this. Let alone acknowledge how much they continue to rely on and depend on them.

"I wasn't born when the 'age of consolidation' happened, but any time I heard my dad talk about it, there was so much sadness in his eyes. Like the world lost some beautiful thing." She glances down at her hands and preens herself by picking possible stray dirt from underneath her fingertips. If Johnny Vinz is listening, he hides it well. He continues driving without diverting his eyes from the road.

"He always hated what I did." She admits sullenly. "As the world turned virtual, my father turned to nature. He said the last thing we need is to be more isolated from people." She lifts her gaze back to the atmosphere outside. "I wonder if he ever saw the irony."

She smiles lightly as the fond memories move into her mind. It has been so long since she'd been reminded of her childhood. There was a time when her history flushed her with her youth. Nostalgic reminders spurred by passing glances at photographs that had once been found sprinkled lovingly throughout her apartment. They had not been able to do so since they migrated to storage boxes in storage rooms of storage facilities. This happened when she decided to convert her apartment into an extension of her office.

Now, sitting in this car alongside some super creation of the most powerful corporation in Chamariko, she finds herself in a blissful state of memory.

It is so soothing to reminisce about her innocent childhood that she nearly forgets the real danger of her situation. Little does she know, she feels the same as Johnny Vinz traipsing through the digital world of Zayyir's homemade computer. It is as if her past washed away the turmoil of her present.

"My dad," Samantha continues, "was just so completely disappointed when I got my job as an analyst." Her gaze turns down remorsefully. "Mom never forgave me for missing his funeral for my job. I was just so busy back then." Her focus returns to the rural atmosphere. "I don't know why I skipped hers. Maybe I was just a coward." The edges of her mouth turn down in a sad frown. The blissful memory of her childhood is now shattered by its darker reality.

I used to be a coward. Samantha reminds herself. The words had slipped unintentionally out of her mouth. But the resonating reality of their truth continues to infest her thoughts. She wants to cry. *Maybe I still am.* Samantha wishes she didn't believe that.

18

The company vehicle containing Samantha and Johnny Vinz parks near the front entrance of an abandoned technological center. There is no sign posted, no gate, and no identifying markers of any kind. One could pass by without noticing the covert building. It appears so mundane. From the perspective of a casual passerby, this is nothing more than a simple warehouse.

Storage facilities were used quite often before cybernetic augmentations became everyday use. Housing equipment became obsolete when the tech giant Advancement Industries monopolized the market. For a time, they were also used to hide innovations' dirty little secrets. Storage facilities only exist for nostalgic mementos that people like Samantha can't bring themselves to throw away or digitize.

They step out of the car, greeted by evening air, and Johnny Vinz leads the way as they walk toward the front doors.

Samantha stares at the building as they approach. "What is this place?"

"A dark facility." Johnny Vinz responds. "It's a compound designed and built to run a single shadow experiment. All findings were shipped to another site, and they disregard this compound when the work is complete."

Samantha notices blemishes across the walls. *This is not from the erosion of time but from abuse.* Her thoughts run through her mind as she stares at the broken building.

"What happened here?"

"That's what we're going to find out." Johnny Vinz answers as they approach the main entrance.

The rundown nature of the building illustrates years of abandonment. Much of the external security equipment is stripped away. Stray wires from holes where the cameras and motion sensors once occupied.

Johnny Vinz sees a translucent hallucination of people being dragged into the technology center against their will. He assumes these apparitions are residual recordings from the security equipment stripped out of the building. Something about it seems eerie. A shutter trembles up the body of the advanced cyborg. Johnny Vinz stumbles over his feet as the strange tingle shivers out of his shoulders.

"What's with you?" Samantha says. She starts to reach out to him but decides against it.

"Something about this place." Johnny Vinz shakes his head. Underneath the glasses on his face, his eyes flash an expression of fear.

"Are we in danger?" Samantha only is only halfway asking Johnny Vinz. She isn't even sure if she should be more afraid of this place or of him.

"I don't think so." He responds, recovering his constitution.

That is not a good answer. Samantha stares at Johnny Vinz with a concerned expression. *If he shows any more symptoms, I will report to Mr. Drake and get out of here.*

They stop at the main entrance of the dark facility. Steel doors are tightly fastened by an electronic seal. The matte finish of the doors is coated with a thick layer of dust and dirt. Samantha opens a panel next to the large entrance. Unfortunately, the screen remains dark despite her attempts to activate it.

"No power." She says, turning to Johnny Vinz. "Without electricity, we can't turn the access panels on and-" Her obvious observation is cut short as the panels suddenly illuminate with power. Moments later, the door opens, revealing the facility's main lobby.

"There's always power somewhere." Johnny Vinz says with a slight smirk as he moves into the lobby of the dark facility.

It must have been residual energy left in the compound. Samantha thinks to herself as she watches Johnny Vinz nonchalantly walk further into the building. *Who the hell is this guy?* Samantha still wonders if she is working alongside a cyborg or a robot. She'd all but convinced herself of her beliefs regarding Johnny Vinz, but every moment seemed to bring a new revelation about this strange individual that she's been paired with. The question is essential. She knows this. At least cyborgs have a human component. Sometimes, she wonders if circuits and wires are under his skin or flesh and bone. It is a question that won't be answered anytime soon. Secretly, Samantha wished she could see his organs working their natural process just to put her mind at ease. She never trusted machines. Perhaps, this is why she chose never to augment herself.

Dark hallways branch out of the main lobby of the technology center. The interior atmosphere is even more disturbing than Samantha witnessed in the exterior.

Signs of slaughter and a scrambled evacuation lead the way to the mainframe room deep in the center of the compound. Spots of dried blood splattered against the walls and on the floor are an ominous revelation. No bodies, though.

The building's interior is trashed, dismantled, and scavenged. Samantha can't be sure if the blood spatter is from the evacuation or skirmishes between scavengers afterward. She shakes her head. *Scavengers don't take their dead with them.*

Computer consoles lie dormant at the center of the lobby. Once filled with flickering lights, the monitors are dead, devoid of power and purpose. The interior of the building shows significantly fewer signs of age. Only a thin layer of dust coats the panels and floors. Aside from the bloodstained patches sprinkled throughout the room, it is pristine. The air purifiers must have been the last to be powered down.

Whoever stripped the technology center did a fast and careless job. Wires hang out of walls where monitors, security equipment, and computers are ripped out in a frenzy, while other areas appear untouched after the seemingly impromptu exodus.

"If the main doors were sealed," Samantha begins, "then how did anyone strip this place?"

"I don't know."

"What happened here?" Samantha continues to question, marveling at the nightmare surrounding her.

"I don't know." Johnny Vinz responds, twisting his head around as he observes his surroundings. "I guess that is what we are here to find out."

"You don't know?" Samantha is shocked, confused, and a little scared. While she found incredible frustration working alongside this freak of technology, she'd always found some comfort in his fantastic knowledge base. However, his ignorance struck her as incredibly disconcerting.

"Hold up." Johnny Vinz stops near the entrance to one of the eerie hallways.

Samantha crouches down as she did when the first rounds of Captain Richard's horrific assault on the military base pierced through its metallic shell and ripped an executive apart in front of her. She is ready to run at a moment's notice. Her heart was already pumping in frenzied anticipation of some technological monster lurking in the darkness.

"What is it?"

Johnny Vinz removes his glasses, revealing closed eyes. He takes a moment to prepare himself, inhales deeply, then opens them slowly.

"I can't see..." He says after a moment. His eyebrows scrunched together in an expression of confusion.

"What?" Samantha stares at him nervously.

"Usually, when I look around, I see everything. All the information pinging off every console."

"What was that like?" Samantha can't hide the impressive nature of his ability. She finds this revelation more interesting than why he stopped her and took his glasses off in the first place.

"It was more than I could handle." He responds, still peering around. "That's why I wear these." Johnny Vinz holds up the glasses toward Samantha. "They reduce the amount of information that I receive. Filter out any unwanted data so I can focus on what is important. But here," he says, continuing to peer at the metallic tomb, "there is nothing to reduce."

Samantha shutters. Now she is scared again. "That's bad."

Johnny Vinz lets out a frustrated sigh. "It means we get to investigate the old-fashioned way until I can get a computer to talk to me."

He leads her down one of the dark corridors. His eyes illuminate as a pair of flashlights to guide their journey.

They stop at a pair of steel doors. Above them, a once-illuminated sign marked 'Main Testing Area' inhibits their progression.

As he did with the main entrance doors, Johnny Vinz reroutes power from an unknown place deep in the facility. The doors energize and open, revealing a strange room. Nothing can be seen. The room is pitch black. The only lighting coming from his eyes.

Samantha stops and holds her hand up. "After you." She enters the room a safe distance behind him.

The expansive testing bay is filled with hundreds of identical neurological testing chairs. Wires and cranial mounts wait for another subject to continue their relentless mission of cognitive infiltration.

Samantha feels a shutter creep up her spine, momentarily causing her head to shiver.

Again, Johnny sees a faint hallucination. **This time, it is an image of doctors milling about the various chairs. Seemingly willing test subjects occupy the chairs and wait submissively to be connected to the machines. Others, who'd already been attached, lay seemingly comatose. Their limbs were tightly fastened to the chairs.**

Monitors spit out readings of brainwaves and other vital signs sent by electrodes attached to the shaven heads of each test subject.

Samantha realizes that her hand is resting on her weapon. She didn't even know she'd been carrying one until now. This place is intimidating. She feels an air of danger surrounding her.

Johnny Vinz puts his hand out to stop Samantha from moving forward.

"I'll let you know when that's necessary." He says in a calming tone.

"Will you?" She says, glaring at him apprehensively. His abilities are not the issue. Her trust in him is the problem.

A desiccated body occupies one of the chairs near the front of the room. Though neither can determine who it is from where they are standing in the room, something about the body feels incredibly important. They move closer to the disregarded carcass.

As they move closer, Johnny Vinz and Samantha see the decomposed corpse of a long-dead test subject.

"Who is this?" Samantha asks, her eyes fixated on the near skeleton. She nervously pushes stray strands of hair behind her ear.

Johnny Vinz retrieves a chart hanging against the side of the testing chair and reads it. Most of the writing is illegible. "Subject twenty-three." He reads as he glances between the chart and the chair with a puzzled look.

"Who was it?"

"A program in Zayyir's apartment mentioned 'subject twenty-three'." Johnny Vinz thinks aloud.

"Do you think Zayyir knew him?"

Johnny Vinz shakes his head and twists his mouth in light contemplation. "Don't know, don't care." He drops the chart back into its place. "Unless it was Zayyir, this 'subject twenty-three' doesn't help us." *I am looking for the source of the virus, not some casualty of progress.* The heartless thoughts casually pass through the mind of Johnny Vinz as he moves back towards the door leading to the hallway connected to the main lobby.

Samantha can't take her eyes off the body. "Well, this person has been here for a few years."

They move back into the corridor and continue toward the mainframe room. At least, that's what Samantha believes.

"What happened to this place?" Samantha repeats aloud, hoping for an answer other than 'I don't know'. *Disregarding a compound doesn't usually leave so much evidence behind and has never been Advancement Industries style.*

"Sudden and violent evacuation." Johnny Vinz responds absentmindedly. "Between the blood spray, the bullet holes, and missing computer components, it appears the security systems must have malfunctioned and started killing everyone."

Samantha can't stop her hands from shaking. Now, she is petrified. "The virus?" *How long has this virus been plaguing us? Or, more importantly, how long has Christian Drake known about this problem?* If Christian Drake hid this virus from so many, even those working for

Advancement Industries, it could only reflect his fear. And anything that Christian Drake fears terrifies Samantha.

"It would explain why there's so little activity here." Johnny Vinz had loaded all of the information that Christian Drake collected on the Mayhem Virus during their cybernetic communication, but still, in all that data, he could not find anything about this facility, nor could he find anything about this 'subject twenty-three' who clearly had something to do with the actions taken by Zayyir. Even with these strange revelations, Zayyir's motives remain an enigma. Johnny Vinz is sure that if he can discover why Zayyir did what he did, he might find himself a step closer to discovering the cure to this horrific plague.

Samantha and Johnny Vinz stop at a dead-end. In front of them lies a large, locked security door marked 'Holding Area'. This area of the facility looks untouched during the exodus.

Johnny glances at his surroundings as if just now coming out of a trance. He glances curiously at Samantha.

"How did we end up here?" He asks.

"I was following you." She responds.

He glares at the magnetically sealed door. A strange wave of emotion washes over his body. His stomach tightens with a queasy feeling.

"Well, let's see what's inside." He decides as he approaches the door. With a slightly timid movement, Johnny Vinz reaches his hand toward the console. He struggles for a moment before the door energizes.

"You can power electronics with your hand?" Samantha isn't sure why she is still allowing him to surprise her. Every moment with Johnny Vinz brings a new revelation about him. It is coming to the point that Samantha wonders how little she knows about the city she's lived in her whole life. *How many other Johnny Vinz' are walking around in Chamariko?*

Rather than answer with a simple 'yes', Johnny Vinz frankly explains his unique ability with one word. "Electromagnetism."

The door shifts and lifts open.

"Great." Samantha begins sarcastically. "Another hallway."

They walk through the door into a ghostly corridor containing multiple holding cells. Five rooms in total line the short hallway, with the last cell capping a mysterious passage like a cul-de-sac. It oddly reminds Samantha of the 'corporate cul-de-sac'. The most important appears to be hidden at the bookend of the corridor.

Nothing about this place is welcoming. On the contrary, it raises Samantha's hair on the back of her head. The stark, flickering lighting flashes ominous shadows in the nooks and crannies of the mid-sized hallway. It smells musky and unwelcoming. Even the silence crowds the hallway with an intimidating presence.

Thick metal doors separate each heptagonal holding cell from the hallway. They peer into the first cell through a clear plastic window with wire stripes to resist any impact from individuals that once occupied the room.

Johnny Vinz continues to stare through the small window of the first door. He hesitates momentarily before grasping the doorknob. There is a strange sense of remembrance. Something about this holding area is familiar to him. It is a sense of being here, living here, in some previous life. *Maybe this is residual data I gleaned from Zayyir's computer programs without realizing it. If he embedded data into his algorithm that I couldn't identify, then he was indeed a genius of historical proportion.* Johnny Vinz starts to turn the steel doorknob.

Samantha notices his pigmentation weakens from its natural ebony hue to one of an ashy gray. Her incessant question about Johnny Vinz's humanity is finally answered with another question. *Robots never lose their color.* She acknowledges. *His sickly pale face proves he has at least some elements of humanity. But what is causing this in him? Why does he look so scared right now?*

"What is the matter with you?" Samantha asks, half reaching her hand out. However, she doesn't extend her arm fully and touch him because she is still slightly afraid of him. Her timid motions are matched with a cautious expression. Johnny Vinz may appear in need, but he is also a highly effective cybernetic organism that could be infected with the Mayhem Virus. With a computer infection this novel, nothing can be taken for granted. *Then again,* she thinks, *if he was infected, standing a few feet behind him is about as safe as watching him point a gun at me.* Even with this acknowledgment, she is in no hurry to help him.

"I don't know." He responds. His voice is shallow and weak. He can feel his internal organs twisting and moving beneath his skin. It is as if his entire body is screaming to run away from this place.

Samantha retrieves a chart hanging from the wall near the cell door. "It says, 'Subject one, Victor'. There is no last name." She flips through the pages of the medical chart. "The chart is blank like the whole thing has been redacted."

Johnny Vinz pushes through the strange feelings of illness and opens the door. Inside the room, beige padded walls with no window are lit by a dull glow of a single fluorescent light in the center of the roof. It is perfectly designed to hold the mentally unstable, although it is ruined by a lack of care and attention. The padded walls are scarred by hysterical attacks from whatever psychotic inmate inhabited it so long ago. Pieces of the padding protrude out of the plastic facade. Age altered the color of the cotton padding to a putrid yellow hue.

Johnny Vinz finishes inspecting the empty room, and they continue to the next door. Before looking inside, Johnny Vinz snatches the medical chart from its container near the second door and reads it aloud.

"Subject two, Innessa."

The room is identical to the first. Lit solely by a single fluorescent light in the center of the ceiling.

"Strange," Samantha admits. "This part of the facility still has power. It must be running from a separate source. I wonder why this place is different from the others."

The chart near the third door reads 'subject three, Nathan.' Scientific markings are etched into the ground on the room's floor. The floors of these rooms consist of thick rubber padding rather than the cotton-filled plastic of the walls.

Johnny Vinz stops at the chart. His expression drops. Standing still in a shivering body, Johnny Vinz stares at the medical chart in shock.

"What?" Samantha asks, reaching for the plastic memorandum. "What is it?" She glances at the information and finds herself wearing the same expression. Then, wiping the illusion from her eyes, Samantha looks back at the name. It reads: 'Subject four, Zayyir'.

"This is it." Johnny Vinz says, his legs wobbling from the shock. He thought nothing could surprise him. He even felt that he'd prepared an expectation of finding Zayyir somewhere in this facility. *So why is this affecting me so much?*

Johnny Vinz glances at the sealed door of the cell that once contained Zayyir.

"The greatest hacker in human history died here."

Samantha shakes her head. "The news reports said that he died jumping off the roof of his apartment building over fifteen years ago. So he couldn't have died here."

Johnny Vinz scoffs. "You believe news reports? They're trained to lie for a living."

Samantha eyes him. There is a hint of hate in his voice.

They move to the last door. Johnny Vinz tries to recover his constitution but staggers toward the final holding cell.

Samantha snatches the plastic medical chart from its place next to the door and reads it. She inspects each of the pages before sharing her revelation with Johnny Vinz. "The name on the chart has been destroyed. It just reads 'subject five', nothing more."

The door is never opened. Johnny Vinz can't do it. As he nears the door, his hands begin to tremble uncontrollably. Faint asthmatic breaths quiver uselessly out of his mouth. His internal organs wrench viciously, and he feels his blood curdle in his veins.

"Something is wrong," He says in a soft whisper.

The overwhelming sensations force him to the ground. Johnny Vinz lands on his hands and knees. Vomit projects from his mouth against the wall and the floor. He barely has enough time to catch his breath before another gush of bile and stomach acid creates a pool in front of him.

Samantha steps away from him in shock, fear, and disgust.

"Johnny?" She calls out helplessly as she watches this masterpiece of technology be reduced to a sickly child. She can see in his expression all confidence drained from him through the moist heaves of regurgitated food and liquid.

"Get me out of here." With his head still hung low, Johnny Vinz blindly reaches up for support. "Please." His look and the feeble sound of his pleading cry desperately spark compassionate terror in Samantha.

She takes him under her arm and carries the technological masterpiece known as Johnny Vinz to safety.

This is more than vulnerability. Samantha can't help but think to herself as she holds him in her arms in their retreat from the holding center of this dark facility. *He is terrified.*

19

Cold water from a running bathroom faucet pools quickly in the hands of Johnny Vinz. His eyes focus intently on the tap water pooled in his hands. Lost in thought, he doesn't move for a long time as water overflows and pours into the sink, circling the drain briefly before disappearing into the dark abyss of the drain.

He quickly brings the liquid up and spreads it across his face. The chilling sensation tickles his senses. He puts his mouth to the falling stream and suctions the aerated fluid into his mouth before spitting the rancid taste of vomit back into the sink.

Light flickers on and off from the ill-powered fluorescent bulbs in the ceiling. Johnny Vinz had rerouted power from hidden locations in the dark facility into the bathroom lighting outlets, but something about the wiring in this restroom failed to work correctly. The inconsistent strobe might have frustrated him if Johnny Vinz wasn't hyper-focused on his current dilemma. It has only been twenty-seven hours since he woke up in that hospital room in the depths of Advancement Industries.

But, unlike a child born, his existence predates his conscious arrival in the world. Waking up was just the final stage of his activation. Johnny Vinz existed long before that moment.

Perhaps, he considers as he watches water continue to fall out of the facet into his hands and out of his hands into the sink and down the drain like an eternal fountain; *this is where some of my code was written. Maybe that is why I'm getting this awful feeling in the pit of my stomach.*

This facility is evil, or at least, it might as well be with the destructive authority it seems to have over him. Johnny Vinz thought his worst sensations were left in the room with that doctor when he endured the pain of connecting nerves, but this feeling even supersedes that horrific experience tenfold.

Something about this place strikes at his core. Some erased memory of a past life. He didn't care about his origin before when searching for Zayyir's whereabouts; perhaps, he still doesn't. His continuous mantra 'don't know, don't care' is becoming increasingly difficult to defend himself. The entire statement hinged on the understanding that knowing his origin did nothing to accomplish his objective; this may not be the case anymore. *If my origin is tied in with this place, I may have to discover myself before locating Zayyir.* Johnny Vinz chuckles. This sounds like some strange fortune cookie nonsense.

The truth is Johnny Vinz had been forced to physically investigate this facility because of careless and destructive scavengers. And now, this psychological breakdown caused by the holding area of this dark facility is forcing him to consider searching inwards to find his answers.

Of course, this couldn't be easy. Johnny Vinz' first mission after waking up is this monstrosity. Johnny Vinz was literally born yesterday, and this is what he must deal with.

Underneath the flowing water, Johnny Vinz can see his fingertips pruning. *How long have I been sitting here?* He wonders before splashing the water on his face and wiping the back of his neck with his moist hands.

He wipes the gross of memory and sickness from his face and the residual water with a rough paper towel. He breathes in deeply, holds it, and releases the stress with a controlled exhale.

Steam rises up, fogging the mirror to a slight haze. Shutting the facet off, Johnny Vinz lifts his eyes from the draining sink and peers at his reflection in the mirror. Johnny Vinz does not see himself reflected back. **Instead of his own mirror reflection in the mirror, Johnny Vinz sees Zayyir staring back at him with a devilish smile from inside the confines of the reflective glass.** Johnny Vinz feels his body tighten suddenly by the reflective interloper; **a movement that is not replicated by Zayyir. The mirage of the youthful hacker continues to stare at Johnny Vinz with the same sinister smile as if waiting for him to regain his faculties. Zayyir stands so still that his image could be a picture.**

"You know, you're going crazy, right?" The childish apparition states, lifting his eyebrows knowingly as he continues holding his sinister smile without breaking eye contact.

In shock and surprise, Johnny Vinz reflexively slams his fist against the mirror. The mirror shatters against the impact of his fist. Pieces of glass tap against the sink and floor with a shower of chiming sounds. They ping against various surfaces and spread around him before slowly settling into place.

Johnny Vinz stares at the shattered glass still connected to the wall, breathing heavily. His face trembles with emotion.

Zayyir's evil presence no longer consumes his reflection. Instead, Johnny Vinz only sees himself in the fragmented pieces of glass on the wall. The jagged edges of the mirror give way to the stainless steel walling of the facility. Johnny Vinz stares at the broken structure of his reflection. A spider web fracture spreads out from the source of the impact.

Lights still flicker on and off, temporarily leaving Johnny Vinz in a dark room with only his confused thoughts to keep him company. The serrated fragments continue to reflect his shocked expression.

Having heard the crashing sound of glass, Samantha rushes into the bathroom. She is scared and alert. Her weapon is drawn, pointed to the side at the ground, and her index finger pressed tightly against the trigger guard.

Her gun hand shows a whitish hue from her tight grip on the handle.

She swivels her head back and forth, observing the bathroom. She sees nothing but an empty room containing only Johnny Vinz, sinks, and stalls. Breathing heavily, she takes another moment to glance around the room before centering her gaze on Johnny Vinz, who continues to stare at his own reflection in a broken mirror. She stands behind him at a safe distance. Staring at the magnificent cybernetic specimen in the fragmented pieces of what used to be an intact mirror, her expression changes to one eerily similar to Zayyir's. Johnny Vinz does not notice the change in her demeanor. He is far too captivated by the strange events that have just unfolded.

"You're infected." Samantha says. Her voice is soft and compassionate. It is almost as if she is pleading with him to recognize his own state of mind.

"What?" Johnny Vinz doesn't turn to her. Instead, he peers down at the fragmented glass pieces collected at the center of the sink just around the drain. The porcelain receptacle is still moist with cold water. An ominous feeling raises the hairs on the back of his neck. Johnny Vinz lifts his eyes from the drain, and they look at each other through the pieces of mirror still desperately clinging to the metal frame mounted on the steel wall.

"You're sick." She reiterates, leaning forward in a slight invasion of his personal space.

"I'm fine." Johnny Vinz shakes his head as he objects. "This place is just doing something to my head. I checked my vitals. Everything looks good." His hands clasp tightly to the sides of the sink. It is as if letting go would result in him floating away from the restroom to some undisclosed place.

Samantha Shaw moves closer; her face hovers over his right shoulder like some disembodied apparition.

"Johnny," she persists, "you are infected with the Mayhem Virus."

"I am not infected!" He protests ardently. The porcelain cracks under the pressure of his intense grip.

Her face changes. She no longer looks at Johnny Vinz with a compassionate expression; but one of spiteful determination. It is an expression of ominous and sinister hatred. As if his refusal to accept her claim creates a sense of hateful rage in her.

She leans away from him. "Then who are you talking to?" Samantha asks before disappearing from his vision like a forgotten memory.

Johnny Vinz alertly looks into the mirror and sees nothing behind him. He spins around to see an empty bathroom. Samantha is not there. She never was. He is, as he always was, alone in the bathroom. Nothing but confusion keeps him company.

Shattered glass still lies around him as a reminder of his psychotic episode resulting in the collision of fist and glass. The bathroom lights continue to flicker on and off,

off and on, on and off. The room is sent into darkness, then brought into the light before returning to the darkness.

Is this the infection? Johnny Vinz wonders in this solitary bathroom with flickering lights and a broken mirror. *Am I infected? Or is this just a repercussion of entering Zayyir's personal computer system at his apartment? Something triggered when I came to this facility. Maybe it's not the infection,* Johnny Vinz continues to contemplate, *but one of the security measures that the child genius left behind.*

There needs to be more evidence to formulate a concrete theory. Not even the great Johnny Vinz, the perfect fusion of man and machine and the prideful innovation of Advancement Industries, can decipher this hallucinatory riddle. Without a resolution, his mind loops and reorders facts to fit the narrative he needs to believe is true.

Johnny Vinz glances down at the fragmented pieces of mirror on the floor surrounding him before he exits the bathroom. His feet crunch against the floor as he walks through the minefield of shattered mirror pieces.

Samantha leans against the wall just outside the door in a girlish posture. She stares down at her hands, wearing a knowing smile. Her fingers are interwoven, and she twiddles her thumbs when Johnny Vinz emerges from the bathroom. Samantha watches him exit the restroom from the corner of her eye. She can't help but let out a slight giggle.

"Everything okay?" She greets Johnny Vinz as he steps into the hallway.

He passes by her without casting a glance in her direction. He is so consumed in his thoughts that he doesn't notice Samantha's devilish smile as he walks past her.

"Let's just get to the mainframe room." He says as he starts down another corridor toward his objective. "I think I can get one of the computers operational and find the last known location of Zayyir."

The answers are in that room. Johnny Vinz tells himself as he continues walking **with Samantha close at his side.** *They have to be.* He cannot admit it, not even to himself, but he is scared, terrified even.

20

Samantha sits nervously in the vehicle provided by Advancement Industries. If she tugged her blonde hair any harder behind her ear, it might rip out of her scalp. Instead, she gently pinches her earlobe and messages it gently. Once in her youth, Samantha remembers hearing that this simple action relieved stress; whether this is true or not, the action seems to be working. Her angst slowly soothes as she sits in this company vehicle.

Oh my god, he's infected. Johnny Vinz is infected with the Mayhem Virus. He's going to go crazy. How long was he infected? Was he always infected? He wasn't showing symptoms until the apartment building, until Zayyir's apartment. Maybe that's when it happened. She remembers thinking this over and over again on her way to the car after guiding Johnny Vinz to the bathroom in the dark facility like some unforgettable mantra that consumed her mind. Samantha has moved beyond fear and concern to terror. *If he is infected,* she continues thinking, *maybe he won't go crazy until he's in a large group of people. Everyone else that succumbed to the infection did so when they were in a crowd.*

Captain Richards at the military complex and Colonel Anders on the streets of Chamariko. Even the incident that James described happened in a group. But if Johnny Vinz goes crazy now, I would be the only casualty. Samantha isn't sure if this is reassuring or horrifying. While it would be good that the body count would be low, she still doesn't want to be the only casualty. She does not want to die, not for Advancement Industries.

The heads-up display anchored in the dashboard of the company vehicle is lit with an image of the robust Christian Drake. His false projection of vibrant health continues to portray the lie of his well-being.

There is silence in the car as Christian Drake contemplates the report that Samantha offered when establishing the link.

Johnny Vinz' recent irrational behaviors are enough to warrant an emergency message to her employer. Samantha knew this seeing him doubled over in the holding area of the dark facility. As soon as the bathroom doors closed behind Johnny Vinz on his way to clean himself up, Samantha bolted for the exit to get to the car Advancement Industries gifted for this mission so she could explain the situation to Christian Drake.

Now, with Christian Drake on the heads-up display, she stares absently at the entrance to the dark facility. Even if she was an organic, Samantha couldn't help but be in awe of Johnny Vinz' abilities. He was a marvel of innovation. The perfect example of all that Advancement

Industries was capable of accomplishing. His infection could only be a testament to the incredible ability of Zayyir. If Johnny Vinz was genuinely infected with the Mayhem Virus, as Samantha believed, it would prove that the youthful prodigy defeated the technological juggernaut after his death.

She grew up being told about the incredible defeat of Zayyir by the altruistic company in defense of society. What she realizes now is terrifying. Advancement Industries did not lie about overcoming the child's assault. They were simply wrong about it.

"Where is he now?" Christian Drake asks, finally breaking the silence.

"I left him in the bathroom. But this couldn't wait." Samantha subconsciously wrings her hands when she responds to his question.

Christian Drake's youthful computerized image nods. He accepts her judgment. The chief executive officer of Advancement Industries always knew that infection was a possibility with Johnny Vinz. A virus capable of infecting all electronics in the world would eventually break through any firewalls that his precious invention could erect.

"You did the right thing in telling me." Christian Drake reassures. "Please, calmly escort Mr. Vinz back here."

She exhales in a sigh of relief. "Of course." It is good to be supported. Samantha secretly believed Christian Drake would treat her like all her other recent encounters, blaming her and trying to intimidate her into whatever action was desired rather than the one that needed to be taken. Her eyes move from the facility's entrance to Christian Drake's image on the heads-up display. "Thank you."

Christian Drake turns his head curiously. "For what?"

"For believing me."

He nods. "Of course, I believe you. This is why you were selected in the first place." His image cuts out, leaving a blank screen with a single Advancement Industries emblem. Samantha leans back in her cushioned chair. Her eyes migrate to the entrance of the dark facility. This place now has an ominous appearance.

Compared to this cybernetic organism, she was next to helpless. Her gaze dropped from Advancement Industries' dirty secret to the firearm she held in her lap. What's the use? Johnny Vinz is the most advanced innovation in all of Chamariko. There is no guarantee that bullets would put him down. He could just as easily upload himself to the network than dodge her attacks with this primitive weapon.

Samantha imagined that for a moment. She shoots this incredible creation, and he moves into the security system to kill her before expanding throughout all of Chamariko. It wasn't that hard to believe. The Mayhem Virus had already made its presence known in a big way.

The orders given by Christian Drake seemed so clear and straightforward, returning Johnny Vinz to

Advancement Industries. But how exactly was she going to accomplish this? What if he resisted? In what world could Samantha Shaw, systems analyst contracted with Advancement Industries, overpower Johnny Vinz, the most significant technological advancement in human history?

She considered these things. Every string of thoughts leads to the same conclusion. Simply tell this terrifying Frankenstein that his creator is calling for him. And if he doesn't listen? Call in the security forces that Advancement Industries is so fond of using. And then leave it to the soldiers to retrieve the weapon.

Her life is more important than their science project.

21

Inside the dark facility, Johnny Vinz enters the mainframe room. Samantha follows close by at his side.

Massive computers line the spherical walls of the large room. This equipment may have once been cutting-edge, but they've become obsolete through the progression of time and innovation. So now they are dormant relics of Chamariko's past.

Johnny Vinz migrates to the control panel and looks over the equipment. *This will require considerably more power than anything I've generated in this facility.* He thinks to himself as he eyes the wall-mounted electronics.

"Now, what will you do?" Samantha asks, calmly standing a few feet behind Johnny Vinz.

He stands in a trance-like state as if operating on autopilot. His eyes, hidden behind the dark glasses on his face, are hazed over.

"I'm going to activate this mainframe."

Samantha's sinister smile grows wider when hearing this. "Good idea."

"There are secrets in here." Johnny Vinz' hands hover over the idle console. He is lost in a stupor. "I have to know what it is before I can accomplish the objective."

He focuses his faculties in search of all sources of power hidden away in the facility. Any dormant energy source must be accessed for him to activate this control panel and find his answers. His questions have grown from simply trying to locate Zayyir to discovering the cause of his strange vomiting episode in the holding area of this facility.

He succeeds in accomplishing his objective. Luckily, there is enough residual energy in the inner recesses of the facility to boot up the archaic technology. Lights on the wall-mounted computing systems flicker several times before lighting with a bold illumination. High-pitched whining sounds can be heard as internal hard drives spin two hundred thousand revolutions per minute. It takes a short time for power to reach the control panel where Johnny Vinz and Samantha stand. Knobs and levers illuminate as power is fully restored to the mainframe room.

I am capable of the equivalent of ten of these gigantic computers. This may have amused Johnny Vinz at one time. If it had not been for his most recent experience, he would find himself smiling. But the terrible situation that he now finds himself in suffocated any humor he may have once had.

Finally, some answers can be discovered. Johnny Vinz thinks to himself as a screen emerges from the opposite side of the control panel. It lifts up from its hiding place nearly twenty inches before locking into position. A moment later, the screen illuminates. The scrolling code lifts up from the bottom of the screen as the system finishes booting up. Once completed, the idle screen pops up, waiting in eager anticipation for a command to be given. Johnny Vinz can't hide his eager jubilation. This journey of strange events starting from his first moments in the hospital room of Advancement Industries has sent him on a roller-coaster of unique experiences culminating in the ejection of his gastric contents.

Samantha watches him eagerly type commands into the computer through the control panel. "Don't worry," Samantha says slightly, with eyes fixated on the back of his head. "You'll have the answer. Everything is a formula. And every formula has a purpose. Right, Nathan?"

Johnny Vinz hears this. The tone and manner strike him. Something about how Samantha spoke reminds him of Zayyir. The way the child prodigy looked at him in the bathroom. The matter-of-fact language the youthful nemesis talked to him.

He spins around to face his companion. He glares at Samantha curiously. She is so calm. A sense of comfort and belonging covers her demeanor. And her smile, that smile, reminds him of the vengeful reflection he'd seen in the bathroom.

Why is she looking at me like that? Johnny Vinz does not have long to contemplate this question. **The entry of** a strange interloper into the mainframe room breaks his moment of thought.

This interloper staggers through the doorway, dressed in garb similar to the riffraff in the alleyway next to the rundown shop that sent him on this wild excursion. It is a female. The thick thighs and protruding breasts create a distinct hourglass shape that can be seen through the heavy, ragged apparel. A small, pointy nose with barely visible nostrils protrudes just above a pair of thin lips pursed tightly as she steadily hobbles into the mainframe room. Her eyes, gray with a hint of green, staring at Johnny Vinz and Samantha Shaw with the same lifeless expression seen in the photographs of Captain Richards after his procedure. It is the vacant look of life harbored in a soulless body.

The female interloper steps, one foot crossing over the other, in a zig-zag manner toward the center of the room where Johnny Vinz and Samantha stand.

With laser focus, Johnny Vinz eyes the interloper in her steady progression toward them. His hand hovers near his sidearm in anticipation. Samantha tracks his gaze and sees the interloper moving in her direction. She apprehensively migrates to the side of Johnny Vinz.

Her eyes focused solely on the interloper.

"Hi." The infected greets in a welcoming fashion. Her hand lifts up in a single delightful wave of respect. She wears a blissful smile as she stumbles toward them. "Are you okay?"

"Yeah, we-" Johnny Vinz cuts Samantha off with a gesture. She stops and glances at him curiously.

"What brings you out here?" He asks in a stern, frigid voice. **His eyes are fixated on the infected interloper, who continues moving toward them.**

"What place is this that nobody knows?" The interloper glances around the mainframe room as if acknowledging the entire dark facility erected by Advancement Industries. "Danger found in rules followed." The tone of her voice fluctuates from low to squeaky high and back to normal as she speaks. Her head shimmies back and forth as if it were held on her body with a flimsy wire. Each stumbling step bounces her skull like a bobblehead on the dashboard of a car traveling over rocky terrain.

Her words are gibberish. A perfect, tell-tale sign of infection. Johnny Vinz does not need to analyze the interloper's vital signs to discover whether she is infected with the Mayhem Virus. Her strange mannerisms and illogical word choice are the only evidence he needs.

Samantha continues to apprehensively watch the interloper slowly migrate closer to them. She may not know definitively if this individual is infected with the Mayhem Virus, but the air of tension in the room is enough to raise the blonde hairs on her arms.

"W-We're fine." Samantha momentarily stumbles over her words. "In fact, this is still a restricted area. So you will have to go back the way you came."

The interloper tilts her head slightly to one side as she gazes at Samantha. "But, if you need courage," the interloper mumbles, "I have help. You should see colors. They're beautiful."

"Turn back, now!" Johnny Vinz orders authoritatively. His hand now pressing against the sidearm, which waits eagerly to enter the conversation with its loud voice. **The infected individual continues stumbling forward. Each foot falls to the outside of the other in a zig-zag pattern. "If you don't need help, then help me."**

Samantha furrows her eyebrows in a confused expression.

"What?" She says, peering back and forth between the interloper and her cybernetic companion.

Johnny Vinz turns his attention to Samantha Shaw. His thumb is now straddling the handle of his sidearm. "We need to get out of here."

"Help me." The interloper produces a gun from his waistband. "Help me. Helps me!" Her voice slowly rises to an ear-piercing screech with the sentence.

Johnny Vinz does not see the world for what it is; instead, it is a vision created for him by his infection from the Mayhem Virus. This false presentation of his surroundings is experienced by all those who succumb to the resourceful computer infection. Everything in his perceived reality is an apparition. In actuality, no one stands at his side. Samantha is nothing more than a figment of his imagination.

He is not alone in the room, however. Standing before him, seen as the female interloper, Samantha stares at Johnny Vinz in a statue-like form. She is stuck in a place like a deer caught in headlights. The fear of her situation overwhelmed any rational thought.

She watches Johnny Vinz free his sidearm from its holster. Samantha puts her hands up defensively before waving them frantically in a futile attempt to gain his attention and break him from his hallucination.

The interloper raises her hand, leveling the small firearm at Johnny Vinz.

"Help me," the female interloper says through her thin lips. "Help me. Help me. Kill me. Kill me. Kill me! KILL ME!!" The statement becomes a recurring mantra.

Terror consumes Samantha's faculties. "It's me," she screams, "Johnny. It's me."

Nothing helps her. Nothing could help her. Johnny Vinz is lost in his hallucination. Hesees a raised gun.

"Get down!" He warns the hallucination at his side. "She's going to shoot!"

"VINZ!!"

This is the last word that Samantha will ever speak. Johnny Vinz pulls the trigger of his handgun, allowing it to utter a single explosive word into the world. The metallic statement pierces through her neck, embedding itself in the steel wall of the dark facility constructed by Advancement Industries.

Samantha falls to the ground in a pool of blood. A wave of shock masks the pain caused by the open wound. The bullet had torn through her jugular and clipped her spinal cord before continuing out the back of her neck. Blood pours into her esophagus. She coughs and gags as the liquid chokes her with every gasping attempt to inhale one more breath. Her body convulses uncontrollably. Her eyes, watering from fear and sadness, dart back and forth in search of a delivering angel to free her of this terrible moment; but only the angel of death greets her. She can't speak, can't scream. Instead, she drowns in her own blood.

"Come on," Johnny Vinz says as he steps over Samantha's body. His foot unknowingly presses into her blood pool, leaving a single red trail of bloody footprints as he continues out of the mainframe room. The body that he still believes is a nameless interloper infected with the Mayhem Virus. "We need to regroup. I need to figure out what the hell is going on."

Samantha is dead. Her death goes unnoticed and unappreciated. Johnny Vinz leaves the compound with a figment of his imagination as it follows him to their next destination.

22

Samantha Shaw lingers near the entry of a hotel room. She maintains the same sinister smile Johnny Vinz saw on her when he left the bathroom in the dark facility. **Ms. Shaw twiddles her thumbs around each other over her interlocked fingers. She watches patiently, her eyes intently trained on her cybernetic colleague.**

It is a small room with only two doors. One leads to the exit, and the other to the toilet. The sink, where Johnny Vinz stands **with his back to Samantha**, sits in the corner of the room in full view of the single bed. A floral bedspread covers the queen-sized mattress. Blue-striped, beige wallpaper covers the walls.

Johnny intently as he cleanses his face. Then, **he looks at Samantha through the reflection of the mirror. She puts her hands to her sides and smiles at him.**

"Something is going on. I can feel it. Is there anything else you can tell me about Captain Richards? Anything that wasn't written electronically?" He asks just before drying his face.

"Nothing that will help you." A smirk slowly spreads across her face as she watches him. Her eyes, vibrant and knowing, her gaze at Johnny Vinz lingers on him with a delightful stare.

"I think we should stay positive." Johnny Vinz needs Samantha in the right frame of mind for the first time since he's met her. After the events at the dark facility of Advancement Industries, Johnny Vinz cannot help but question his frame of mind. His organic companion is the control of his mind. Being incapable of infection is now the only element he can rely on in this equation. But for this to work, Johnny Vinz requires Samantha to be in the right state of mind. The way she is acting now is not something he wants to see. It only makes him question his reality even more.

Her smile widens from ear to ear. "You can't win."

Something about her voice catches his attention. Johnny Vinz gazes at her with new eyes. He sees a uniquely strange change in her personality.

"Why not?" He asks, his eyes intently trained on his companion. Looking at her, **he notices a droplet of blood trickling down her neck. The blood drops down onto her clothes. A steady spread of red reaches out from the contact point, staining her white button-up blouse.**

"You're bleeding." He notes, **staring at the small red streak that reaches from the center of her throat, just to the right of her jugular, ending in the spot of discolored fabric.**

Samantha waves her hand dismissively. "That stopped a long time ago." Besides moving her mouth, Samantha stands like a statue as she speaks. Her expression suddenly hardens into an intense stare that pierces through him. It is a burning glare of hatred and determination.

Johnny Vinz stares at Samantha, still confused. His mind runs through scenarios. First, this could just be another illusion discouraging him from reality. Johnny Vinz refocuses his attention on the small streak of blood as it spreads a bloody, maroon stain that begins reaching her shoulder.

"What are you talking about?"

"You killed me." Her statement is so cold and emotionless. It sends a chill up Johnny Vinz' spine.

Johnny Vinz feels his mind breaking in a fleeting moment of shock. He quickly turns back to the sink, jaw hanging open in complete dismay. His hands clasp onto the counter-top as he'd done in the bathroom of the dark facility created by Advancement Industries. His eyes vacantly stare into the dark holes of the covered drain as if some answer can be found in the black recesses of the pipes that lead away from the apartment into the submerged sewers running under Chamariko.

"I can figure this out." He reassures himself desperately. "I can still figure this out."

Samantha's sinister smile returns. "Do you really think you're thinking rationally?" She asks in an evil tone.

Johnny Vinz removes his protective glasses and gazes at himself in the mirror; his bloodshot eyes peer desperately back at him.

"I killed you." He admits to himself.

Samantha nods deliberately. "Shot me, dead."

"I'm infected with the Mayhem Virus." He is finally ready to accept his illness.

She laughs. "You sure are."

"If I'm infected," he starts to rationalize, "then maybe, I can backtrack the Mayhem Virus to its origin through the files in my mind. Something in there has to point me in the right direction."

Samantha curiously tilts her head to one side. She is a figment of his imagination; therefore, she knows what he is thinking. "Hacking into your own mind? A risky proposition."

Johnny Vinz ignores her. She is nothing but a phantom. An apparition designed by the Mayhem Virus to inhibit him from his objective. *Don't believe anything that ghost says. She's not here to help you. She will only confuse you more.*

With his decision made, her voice is nothing more than a hindrance. Johnny Vinz closes his eyes, sets his protective glasses safely to the side where a sudden jerk will not damage them, and prepares himself to hack into the recesses of his own consciousness. When he eyes his open, Johnny Vinz intently gazes into the eyes of his reflective doppelganger in the mirror.

As he did in Drake's office, Johnny Vinz hacks into the computerized system of his own mind.

23

Johnny Vinz opens his eyes. He is back in the decrepit holding area of the technology center erected by Advancement Industries, but the dark facility is different. Sparks flicker from open wires dangling from the roof and walls. Power seems to be coursing through the compound. The five cells of the subject area line the hallway that he stands in. As in the confines of Christian Drake's mind, the surfaces of this place are distorted and unreal. Buffering takes significantly less time to be completed. Johnny Vinz can't be sure if this is because he is more advanced than Christian Drake or if it is because this is his mind that he is hacking into.

Spawning in the facility designed to house the dirty secrets of Advancement Industries was not an expectation for his trip into the virtual world of his own reality. Johnny Vinz engaged in this journey without much thought except to solve this enduring mystery. He may have been more comfortable waking in the office of Christian Drake. A slight desire to see the broken body of the corporate genius bound to his incredibly important chair felt betrayed by the reality of his virtual surroundings.

What the hell? He wonders, his internal voice seeming to echo in the recesses of his mind. He scans his surroundings. Besides the stark angles of sacred geometry on each surface, an ominous presence seems to fill the virtual world. The eerie omnipresence lingers on every surface like a bad odor; more palpable than when he walked through the hallway in real life, and this concerns him. The result of his hallway experience in the real world resulted in him doubling over and vomiting his sanity onto the floor.

Johnny Vinz moves from his place in the hallway toward the first door. His steps echo in the synthetic atmosphere with a ghostly tone. He approaches the first door. The one that had been assigned to Victor in the real world. Johnny Vinz reads the name on the notepad that hangs from the wall near the door to the first holding cell of this hallway. The name, as it did when he first visited this nightmarish place, reads Victor. This time, however, there is a last name. Johnny Vinz cannot make out the last name. The words are blurred out as they would be in a dream. Something in him or this program found within him will not allow the namesake to be discovered. Johnny Vinz moves his gaze from the notepad and peers through the observation window into the holding cell. The padded room is no longer empty.

A sole occupant ritualistically lifts himself up and lowers back down close to the floor in a slow and steady series of push-ups. Each time he rises to the full extension of his arms, he screams another number.

"One fifty-two! One fifty-three!" Beads of sweat drip off his face, forming a pool just under his head.

Victor notices Johnny Vinz peering at him through the window. He jolts up from the floor and stands at militaristic attention, his right hand rigidly pressed against his forehead just above the eye..

"Sir, I am at your disposal, Sir!" Victor hollers as if living in the expectation of boot-camp.

Does he know where he is? Johnny Vinz wonders, staring at the soldier through thick glass that separates the two. *Perhaps he does not see this place for what it is. Like someone that cannot tell they are living in a virtual world.* Johnny Vinz shakes his head, quickly. Thinking such thoughts, questioning one's reality, is a dangerous way to live. Many have justified an incredible number of actions after questioning the validity of their surroundings. *This could be the most dangerous part of the Mayhem Virus. It forces everyone to question the truth, their truth. With this virus playing tricks on the minds of the enhanced, truth and reality do not exist. They are the figment of everyone's imagination. Reality is something discovered in the eye of the beholder. And everyone around them suffers for that fact.*

Johnny Vinz stares at this soldier, trapped in the abyss of a program. The only indication of Victor existing is a single name on a notepad in a nameless facility designed by Advancement Industries to be forgotten. *This soldier appears content.* Johnny Vinz thinks. *He doesn't seem to be dismayed at all by his current place. He seems at peace. Why does he look familiar? I know he is a stranger. My only introduction to this person was the notepad that Samantha read from; and yet, there is a strange air of recognition.*

Victor holds this erect stance until Johnny Vinz disappears from the observation window and returns to his calisthenics. He continues to hone a body that does not exist for a fight that will never come.

Johnny Vinz, moving from the first holding cell to the second, peers into the observation window of the holding cell that now contains Innessa. She is starkly beautiful. Such bold features that, on their own, are unremarkable. The way they come together, and the way she peers at him are so striking, it moves Johnny Vinz emotionally.

Innessa. Johnny Vinz thinks to himself as the two hold a locked gaze. There is nothing gentle about her, but everything is seductive. *Innessa the spy. How do I know this? How do I know her?* Johnny Vinz believed he'd be transported to some strange virtual reality contrived by the Mayhem Virus, or a fail-safe atmosphere constructed by Christian Drake and Advancement

Industries. Now, he is beginning to believe this virtual world belongs to him. *But if this is my reality, who are these people and why are they here?*

Innessa continues to stare quietly at Johnny Vinz from a seated position. Legs folded and hands clasped together in her lap, she watches him with a blank gaze that is strikingly intense. Johnny Vinz moves on to the next holding cell. He is grateful that the sick twisting in his stomach does not crush his internal organs as it did in the real world.

Such a sad scene displayed in the third window. An old man gently rocks back and forth, whimpering and whispering to himself. His arms are bound tightly to his chest by a straitjacket. Teary eyes lifting from the ground, Nathan looks at Johnny Vinz with a broken expression.

Victor simply says, "I used to be a professor." He returns his eyes back to the ground, back to where they belong.

There is no need to linger at this window. Johnny Vinz thinks to himself. *Whatever reality this man lives in, it is one of Hell. There is no need to be part of it.*

Johnny Vinz moves on from the depressing display to his objective. It is the fourth holding cell. The cell that had once contained the greatest hacker ever to grace Chamariko by his presence. A child who sought to challenge the authority of Advancement Industries. The one went from child to savior in his absence. An entire underbelly living on the prophecy of his return. A belief that elevated actual disagreement to possible rebellion. It is the cell that held Zayyir.

He peers into Zayyir's cell through the observation window to see nothing. Zayyir is not inside his cell. He is nowhere to be found.

Confused, Johnny Vinz reaches out and gently pushes on the entry to the empty holding cell. The door is opened with a loud click. Johnny Vinz steps through the threshold and into the cell.

The holding cell in the dark facility of Advancement Industries is not the holding cell in the dark facility of Advancement Industries. When he enters, Johnny Vinz discovers new surroundings. No longer in the technology center, he now stands in Zayyir's apartment.

Johnny Vinz feels another wave of excitement waft over his being. The expectation of a padded room dissipating with the reality of his surroundings. Nothing makes sense. Not even in the digital world of his own mind. *Is this me?* He thinks with the same echoed internal monologue. *Did I enter a program in my mind? Or is this some digital design in Zayyir's computer? Was I ever here? Was I ever in the dark facility? Did I ever leave Zayyir's apartment? Or am I still standing there, in the bedroom of the dead hacker? Staring at a computer screen, locked in a virtual reality created by the nine year old.* Johnny Vinz shakes his head. *This is dangerous. Don't start questioning yourself, or your reality. It is a path to insanity. It is submission to the Mayhem Virus.* Still, he is forced to admit to himself that the strange events that have started to plague him began after hacking into the home-made computer in the outskirts of Chamariko.

Standing at the entrance to Zayyir's bedroom, Johnny Vinz sees a youthful child sitting at the computer. He instantly recognizes the young boy motionless at his desk. No longer disabled or weathered by years of neglect, the home-made masterpiece appears as it did before the prodigy's capture.

The multiple screens of his magnificent computer system illustrate the various programs that run on the mainframe. As before, Advancement Industries are the primary focus of his attack. The Advancement Industries emblem is boldly presented on one of the screens facing Johnny Vinz. Most of the programs appear to be designed to infiltrate and attack all of the technologies throughout Advancement Industries. For a moment, Johnny Vinz entertains the idea that the child still lives, guiding the Mayhem Virus in its destructive incursion.

Johnny Vinz does not move. He simply stares apprehensively at the child who sits as a stone.

Zayyir feels the presence of Johnny Vinz behind him. Without turning, he simply looks over his computer. His hands hover over the small keyboard that enacted such a devastating blow to the powerful corporation. To the entire city of Chamariko.

It is strange to think. Everyone viewing this child as a saving grace for the city. The reality being a terrifying virus that threatened the stability of all living in their advanced city. Is this liberation? Would the city of Chimariko really be saved by dismantling everything that made it great? Johnny Vinz shutters at the thought. This couldn't be the work of a liberator, but a destroyer.

"I was sitting right here when it happened." The boy says, glancing down at his hands in a look of remembrance. "They smashed through the door and then..." Zayyir trails off momentarily. Feeling the final moments of his childhood. "This was the last place that I was alive." He smiles slightly. Not a sinister smile filled with hatred and malice. It is an expression of content admiration. "And to think, this is the place that I won."

Johnny Vinz eyes Zayyir with cautious curiosity. "Why did you kill Samantha?"

"She served her purpose." He answers coldly. "Besides, I didn't need her stopping you. She was an organic. A variable that I did not need to contend with."

"Stopping me from what?"

Zayyir swivels in his chair, stopping the seat just as it faces Johnny Vinz. "From entering here." He says in a matter-of-fact manner. "Stopping you from hacking into your own mind. Hell," he chuckles, "even the hallucinated version of Samantha that I created tried to warn you."

The one who stood by me as I murdered my organic companion. Johnny Vinz steps forward assertively. "How did you get into my brain?"

Zayyir nods with a slight smirk and shakes his head. He is not a child. His mannerisms are proof of this. But his response to Johnny Vinz' question is one given to a stupid and obvious question. "That is a difficult question to explain." He sighs. "But, first thing is first."

Moving at inhuman speed, Zayyir leaps from the chair and latches onto Johnny Vinz faster than any reaction can be made. Johnny Vinz is incapable of defending himself.

He finds himself submerged in water. It is as if the moisture of his synthetic surroundings gathered into an orb of liquid around his head. Held in place by artificial elements. He struggles against it but cannot free himself from the hallucinated attack.

As Johnny Vinz submits to his terrifying predicament, Zayyir stares distantly at the greatest creation ever devised by Advancement Industries. There is no emotion in his gaze. No hate. No love. Nothing. He seems to view Johnny Vinz as nothing more than another piece of equipment. Perhaps, the same way he viewed Samantha.

"It all started with an equation," Zayyir begins. He stands over Johnny Vinz who collapses on the ground in twisted torment, drowning the imagined liquid.

The cyborg lies on his back with a horrified expression as he gasps for air. He feels the liquid invading his lungs with a burning pain of rejection.

"The problem being: 'the nervous system equation'. How to fuse an organic nervous system with an electronic one."

Zayyir continues to glare down at Johnny Vinz who struggles against his liquid restraint. There is no container. The water simply sits perfectly in place around Johnny Vinz' head.

"Relax." Zayyir consoles, the sinister smile now emerging on his lips, slightly exposing his childish teeth. "The thing about drowning in your own mind is that you never die. So," he continues, "back to what I was saying." Zayyir returns to his seat. "You wouldn't believe how many times they tried, unsuccessfully, to combine the two." He stares at Johnny Vinz.

Even in his state of imagined immersion in the liquid, Johnny Vinz appears confused. He stares at the boy. His body shivers and convulses in pain and fear.

"Okay. They tested on an average of twenty-five thousand six hundred and thirty-nine people per phase." Zayyir waves his hand dismissively. "That is, despite what their official reports said. We were the only success story in phase six. I guess you could call us the sixth subject. We were Christian Drake's mathematical solution to the nervous system equation."

Johnny Vinz cannot reach up to his face and push the water away from his mouth. His arms lock at his sides in a convulsing seizure. He is having a grand-mal-seizure.

Zayyir notices this. "Looks like we're ready for the next step." Zayyir says with a nod. He drags the cyborg's body telepathically to the computer and produces a pair of electrodes from his desk.

"Long story short," he continues, "the answer to the nervous system equation is more organic nervous systems. You see, organic nervous systems think in terms of layers. When you weigh your options, you do not simply think in terms of yes or no. You think about the possible ramifications of the choices and the theoretical outcomes of each choice. A synthetic nervous system can only think in terms of yes and no, ones and zeroes. The answer to this problem was to layer various organic nervous systems so that could weigh options organically. After doing this, they could render a decision to something simple. They would produce a clean yes/no statement for the synthetic nervous system to translate." Zayyir leans forward and stares at an expression filled with hurt. It is the look of painful desperation. "Basically, they killed my body and put me into your brain to act as a bridge for the program living there."

Johnny Vinz continues to struggle futilely against his imagination. He is drowning, but not dying. This experience is worse than anything he has ever felt before. It is worse than the hospital room in Advancement

Industries. It is an experience that makes him wish he were dead.

"They took out your subconscious and replaced it with me... with us. The subconscious is an automated system. But so too is the electronic nervous system." Zayyir stares directly into Johnny Vinz's eyes. "They killed you, Johnny. They killed all of us. And they did all of it in the name of advancement."

Zayyir holds the electrodes ominously above Johnny's eyes. "Just remember," he says gleefully, "this is all in your head."

Zayyir violently jabs the electrodes into Johnny Vinz's eyes. The pain is beyond measure. It is a piercing agony that sears fire into his brain. An excruciating experience like burning white-hot pokers into the core of one's head.

Johnny Vinz stands alone in the hotel room. He steadily loosens his hands from the counter-top. His eyes are still focused on the pupils of his reflected doppelganger. But it is no longer Johnny Vinz who stares into his reflection. Hidden behind the pleased expression, Zayyir now controls the body. He reaches up and gently touches his face. It is the first physical sensation that he's experienced in over a decade. The feeling of a physical body pleases him considerably.

"Zayyir," he says through a broad smile that exposes his teeth. "You don't look like yourself at all." He reaches over near the wall on the counter-top to retrieve his glasses, designed to reduce his awareness of the technological atmosphere surrounding him when traversing the world. Placing the dark glasses back over his eyes, he chuckles before turning away from the mirror and leaving the hotel.

Locked deep in the confines of his own psyche, Johnny Vinz scans his surroundings. It appears that he's been returned to the technology center, though this version of the subject holding cells is layered deeper in the program hidden in the program of his mind.

Padded walls of the cell's interior surround him. A prisoner in his own body, he is an inmate of an insane asylum. His arms are bound tightly in a straitjacket, just as he saw with Nathan before his confrontation with Zayyir. He momentarily struggles against his restraints but ceases his attempts when each movement only succeeds in tightening the thick fabric that binds his arms to his body.

Though he is alone in this padded room, Johnny Vinz does not appear to be by himself. A whimpering sound of a broken man bleeds through the wall. Nathan quietly sobs somberly in the next room.

Nothing in the cell appears natural, even less so than first traversing the digital world of his mind. Every surface binds to each other in a strange, inexplicable manner. It is reminiscent of the virtual cabin he'd seen when hacking into the files in Christian Drake.

Johnny Vinz tries to move from his seated position against the padded wall, but shackles attached to the

floor hold his feet in one place. Finally defeated, he leans his back against the pillowed wall.

He scoots close to a vent that seems to materialize in his necessity. He leans his face against the downward-facing slats of the grate that cover a duct that leads to Nathan's cell.

"Hey," he calls through the metal and fabric into Nathan's room. "You there." Suddenly, Nathan appears nestled against the wall in the corner of the cell with Johnny Vinz. Nathan's eyes are down-turned in a broken expression of desperation.

The elderly man slowly rocks back and forth in a self-soothing manner. A mixture of gray and black hairs curl out of his scalp in scraggly waves. His tragic eyes, hidden by his lids as he stares intently at the floor, are reddened by excessive crying. He wears a two-piece, navy blue suit with a baby blue dress shirt. A thin, black-striped tie reaches down to his belt. His clothes are worn and crumpled.

"What?" Nathan asks in a shaky voice without making eye contact. Sadness permeates every aspect of his being. His face looks worn and beaten. His hands were hidden in his lap. His shoulders slumped so far that his chest may collapse at any moment.

Johnny Vinz is struck by the sudden appearance of his new cellmate. This feeling of shock brings with it a hint of anger. Someone must be to blame for his evident lack of preparedness. He is the most extraordinary man/

machine hybrid in human history, and they never gave him a handbook on navigating his own mind or what to expect if he may need to enter it.

He adjusts to face his new cellmate, pushing against the floor with his bare feet to pivot on his rear end.

"Who are you?"

Nathan's eyes lift. He gazes around the room. His defeated expression maintains as his head turns from right to left. There is a strange presence of acknowledgement in his eyes.

"I designed this place," Nathan admits, staring at the far end of the padded room.

Johnny Vinz furrows his eyebrows and tilts his head with curiosity. He tries unsuccessfully to make eye contact with his broken cellmate, who stares intently into nothing. "This?"

Nathan nods somberly. "The interface system that binds our individual consciousnesses into this creation. I created the interface. All of us are here because I did my job."

Johnny Vinz shakes his head. He is in the same position as Samantha was when speaking to him. Having a companion answering his questions in a way that leaves him wholly lost, Johnny Vinz feels frustration bubbling from his bowels. "What the hell are you talking about?"

Nathan stares up at the fictitious lights on the ceiling. "I solved the nervous system problem." He says tearfully. "And this is my reward."

"How do I get out of here?"

"You don't," Nathan answers with a head-shake wearily. His eyes return to the floor. "Like the rest of us, you are his slave now." A presence outside of the padded room sends a cold chill crawling up his spine.

Zayyir's face appears in the observation window. "Don't worry." He says from behind the door. His voice was muffled by the thick glass. "This was always going to happen."

Johnny Vinz stares at him with a burning intensity. Hatred forces a tremble in his body. "What's going to happen?"

Johnny Vinz, who is not Johnny Vinz but Zayyir, drives the company car supplied by Advancement Industries. He looks at himself in the rear-view mirror with a satisfied smirk. He can't stop looking at himself. Two dreams will soon be fulfilled.

The first, made as a nine-year-old child in a small apartment with his father, reveals the sinister actions of the most powerful corporate conglomerate in Chamariko. That innocent child never sought to destroy Advancement Industries. Even when constructing his incredible program, he only wanted to demonstrate to the people what their godly overlords did behind closed doors. His evil desires only emerge after witnessing the murder of his father and being captured by the security forces of Advancement Industries. It was years after that moment that his second dream occurred. To enact his vengeance against Christian

Drake and all the executives that helped him in his evil endeavors through their sycophantic actions.

It has been so long since he's inhabited a living body, even if that body is a cyborg.

"I am going to kill Christian Drake." He answers as he continues to drive the vehicle. "And then, I'm going to tear down the rest of Advancement Industries." He glances around, admiring his surroundings. "You have no idea how long I was trapped behind your eyes. Always thinking, always remembering who I was, unable to do anything but what I wanted. Don't know. Don't care. Don't cut it." His expression turns to one of intense anger. "I have plans. I know. I care."

He goes quiet momentarily, listening to Johnny's rebuttal in his mind. It is an internal dialogue. As if he were thinking thoughts to himself. "It is not a virus." He answers. "I found Advancement Industries' idea for this dirty little secret when they conceived it electronically. Part of their program was mind control. Just a young child stumbling onto a terrible conspiracy. Part of their program was mind control. One of the dirtiest of their secrets was a back door that allowed them access to any program they built. So, when Advancement Industries announced brain augmentation, naturally, I was concerned. When I found one of their programs regulated chemical and electrical impulses, I decided to add a modifier to the program. A back door to their back door."

He laughs. "And not a moment too soon. They snatched me up less than a week later. When I first woken up in your mind, we were still hardwired to the network. Just for a moment. Just long enough to send a single message to the artificial intelligence that I implanted into the coding. 'I'm here'. The rest was the program problem-solving."

Johnny continues to stare at Zayyir's computerized face in the observation window. He struggles against his restraints, but his muscles don't respond to his commands. "You killed those people."

"You mean those suicides." Zayyir appears amused. Their deaths are a joke to him. Simple casualties in the war of technological advancement, just as he was.

"So, what's your plan? Punish everybody?"

Zayyir chuckles. "I honestly do not know why the program did that. But, then again, artificial intelligence can be predictably unpredictable."

"All this because you couldn't get your way?" Johnny growls.

Zayyir looks at him. His amusement has dissipated, leaving only resentment. "Something has to change. I tried to change policies peacefully, and they murdered me for it. Now, I will create a power gap forcing Advancement Industries to crumble. And when that happens, everything changes, peaceful and otherwise."

His car halts at a red light. A brief moment of reflection before starting down the final street toward his final goal. Vehicles stop around his car, all waiting to continue their journey to various destinations, none realizing the terrible entity they are stopped next to.

This will be the last moment of tranquility. Once Zayyir completes his statement, the corporate system will be decimated, and everything will be different. Just as he wanted. A vengeful strike against the most powerful corporation in Chamariko from a long defeated adversary. This death blow sought to break the grip of Advancement Industries and create an opportunity for the change that Zayyir had yearned for since his days as a nine-year-old hacker.

24

The light turns green, and cars accelerate through the intersection. Johnny Vinz, who is not Johnny Vinz but Zayyir, adjusts the rear-view mirror once again to get a better look at himself. Vanity never used to be a distinguishing characteristic, but living without a body for over a decade changed that. Now he can't see himself enough. The feel of the company vehicle's leather seats fills him with a sensation not felt since his days as a nine-year-old hacker. This child, now grown into a vengeful adult, cannot help but enjoy the brilliant phenomenon of incredible feelings that fill his senses.

Part of him worries about getting into an accident. Yet, strangely, even with everything on the road outside his vision, he is still distinctly aware of every object surrounding him. This incredible sensory perception reminds the childhood hacker, who commands the cybernetic organism created by Advancement Industries, of that small invention he'd used when trying to escape with his father from their apartment building so long ago. The ability has been up-scaled and enhanced from his nine-year-old science project.

It makes sense. His hand-held sensor identified targets using residual information shared by nearby electronics. Simply put, Zayyir created a component to track people, not just through their electronics, but through the very augmentations inserted into their bodies. This incredible design had been one of the only inventions he didn't have the chance to destroy before his capture.

Advancement Industries must have retrieved the equipment after taking him into custody and reverse-engineered the technology to be incorporated into their Vinz Project.

Zayyir couldn't be sure of this. His memory disappeared after his thirty-story drop from his apartment rooftop. The final moments of his first life seared into his memory with the intense emotions that swirled through his childish fall as wind had rushed passed during his descent. But that was nothing more than a distant memory. Now he has a mission that does not involve self-sacrifice. His objective is retaliation. It involves the collapse of the greatest corporation in Chamariko starting with the death of its debilitated leader. It involves the murder of Christian Drake.

"Christian Drake isn't just the Chief Executive Officer, but the brainchild behind the Vinz Project. This could be the last chance we have before they control everything." He pauses for a moment, eyes still focused on his reflection in the rear view mirror. A sudden realization enters his mind. "Which reminds me."

He reaches toward the dashboard console and opens a communications link to Advancement Industries. The image of a lowly security guard appears on the screen.

Security personnel on these dashboards are glorified secretaries. Yet, somewhere along the line, Advancement Industries felt that having authority figures on their communication channels would present a more comforting display for consumers.

The pleasant image of Alon appears in the console. "Hello there, and welcome to Advancement Industries. My name is Alon, and I am the 'All Information' kiosk of this expansive corporate building. I am here to assist you in any way I can, whether that be answering questions, providing information, or connecting you with the appropriate representative. " she begins, "Hello there, and welcome to Advancement Industries. My name is Alon, and I am the 'All Information' kiosk of this expansive corporate building. I am here to assist you in any way I can, whether that be answering questions, providing information, or connecting you with the appropriate representative.

"Additionally, I can assist you with scheduling appointments, providing directions, or any other tasks that may come up during your call. Whatever your needs may be, I am here to help.

"Thank you for choosing Advancement Industries. How may I assist you today?"

"Hello Alon, my name is Samantha Shaw. I am calling for Christian Drake." Johnny Vinz, who is controlled by Zayyir, says in the voice of the deceased Samantha Shaw.

"Hello Samantha, it's nice to meet you. As the 'All Information' kiosk of Advancement Industries, I can certainly assist you with connecting to Mr. Drake's office, if he's available.

"May I have more information about the purpose of your call, so that I can better assist you? Alternatively, if you already have an appointment scheduled, I can provide you with directions to Mr. Drake's office, as well as any other assistance you may require during your visit."

"I'm calling to update Mr. Drake on the status of Johnny Vinz."

The image of Alon nods delightfully. "Certainly, I can help you with that. As this matter concerns security, I can connect you with one of our security officers who can further assist you via a video call. Please hold while I connect you to the appropriate video line."

"You've reached the Advancement Industries security desk. How may I assist with your call?" The officer asks in a straightforward, unenthusiastic manner.

"This is Samantha for Mr. Drake." The security officer has no idea of the truth. And how could he? On his screen, he sees a delightful woman on the other end of the line. Nothing indicated to him otherwise. The powerful algorithms the cybernetic organism uses rival anything in Advancement Industries, including those found in Christian Drake's office.

"One moment, please." The screen freezes while the security officer sends a request to Christian Drake. Typically, this would never happen. But Samantha has a special clearance.

The elderly invalid sits idly in his advanced chair, watching the multitude of screens. He is fixated on a single video that he plays repeatedly. Not much is shown in his decrepit expression. The disease took his muscle control long ago.

He receives a message. "Samantha is on the line for you." The security officer reports. He can see nothing when speaking to the head of the company but a computer-enhanced image.

"Thank you." Samantha's face appears on a screen directly in front of Drake. "It is good to hear from you, Samantha." Drake's robotic voice greets her.

"Yes. Are you on site?" She responds.

Such an odd question. It just seems out of Ms. Shaw's character. "Why do you ask?" As Christian Drake continues his conversation with this individual, his computer scans every knowable aspect of her persona. He hoped to discover the truth behind this apparent illusion.

No consideration is given to the possible deadly fate that may have befallen Samantha Shaw. She is, or was, an expendable asset Christian Drake used to benefit Advancement Industries. There were millions of organics just like her to be found throughout Chamariko. There was only one Johnny Vinz.

Nothing changed Christian Drake's plan. He still needed his masterful creation to return. It would be the only way to properly decommission him. Even if he suspected this to be a deception, nothing changed anything. If he had been infected by the Mayhem Virus, algorithms and programs were installed into his hardware to create a type of electronic antibody that Advancement Industries could use to put this terrible nightmare to bed.

"I sent Johnny Vinz to Advancement Industries."

Her responses are increasingly disturbing. She speaks as if to have no clue about their previous conversation. "You did?"

She nods. "Your creation discovered the origin of the Mayhem Virus. Are you on site?"

"Yes," Christian Drake answers plainly.

Samantha Shaw smiles. "He should be there soon."

"Thank you." As Samantha disappears into a blank screen, Drake opens a connection back to the security desk.

A younger, more exuberant security officer answers the call.

"Have security ready to recall the Vinz project." Drake begins. "I want him in custody as soon as he steps on Advancement Industries property."

Christian Drake returns to the video. He sees a security feed from the technology center. It portrays Samantha

Shaw's execution. For the first time in his life, Christian Drake fears the future.

Johnny Vinz is still trapped in the deep confines of his own subconscious. The walls shift in a glitchy manner. He turns back to Nathan. The pathetic scientist continues to whimper. "How do I get out of here?" Johnny asks. This man may be broken, but he is also the best chance Johnny has of escaping this virtual prison.

"I used to be a professor." Nathan continues his mantra, weeping quietly.

"Hey!" Johnny jolts him with the intensity of his voice. "Then teach me how to get out of here."

Nathan stops moaning for a moment. He considers Johnny's question. "You are your prisoner." He answers. "In your mind, nothing is real and everything is possible."

Johnny tries to understand Nathan's cryptic answer. "So, if I believe that I can overpower him and take control of my body, then I can?"

"Not that simple." Nathan shakes his head. "You need to make him believe it." He gestures to Zayyir whose face still appears in the observation window. The young hacker can see them, but he cannot seem to hear them.

"How do I do that?"

Nathan finally makes eye contact with Johnny. "You entered here as the admin and Zayyir hacked into control. Therefore, to get control..." he trails off.

"I have to hack the admin." Johnny understands.

Johnny Vinz, who is not controlled by Johnny Vinz but Zayyir, steps into the bustling lobby of Advancement Industries. Various representatives and security agents meander through the large, elegantly designed corridors. They walk to various destinations, completely oblivious to the terrible tragedy soon to befall their organization. He moves around a careless crowd on his way to the security terminal.

The delightful image of Alon appears in her kiosk near the front doors of the building. "Welcome back, Ms. Shaw! I recognize you from our previous video call. I see that you have a meeting scheduled with Mr. Christian Drake on the top floor of the Advancement Industries building. Would you like me to provide directions to the elevators that will take you there?"

A smile widens on the ebony face of Johnny Vinz. *This stupid AI program still sees Samantha Shaw even though it is looking right at me.* "No. I think I have it from here."

"Certainly. It was a pleasure assisting you today. Remember, if you have any further questions or concerns, please don't hesitate to visit me at any of my kiosks throughout the building. And always remember our Advancement Industries slogan: Always succeeding, always advancing. Thank you for choosing Advancement Industries."

A heavy-set security guard mans the post. He glares up from the security monitors set in his desk and rubs the thick beard that covers his face as he watches Vinz approach him.

"Good afternoon, Sir." The security guard greets. He recognizes Johnny Vinz but does not know that it is, in fact, Zayyir who controls the body. How could he? There is, however, a 'detain immediately' authorization for Vinz. The security guard knows this. As he greets Johnny, he presses a hidden button to signal a silent alarm.

"Is Mr. Drake in?" Johnny Vinz asks in a cold manner. A flickering expression of snarling disgust flashes across his face.

"You are?" The security guard knows who he is, he's just buying time.

Vinz gazes at the computers that fill the lobby. "I'm here to see Mr. Drake. Is he in? There seems to be quite a bit of interference."

"Of course, just have a seat." *Come on, where are you guys?* The guard thinks.

"So, he's in the building?" Vinz continues to scan his surroundings.

"We'll call you when we're ready."

Vinz' gaze fixates on a single spot on the ceiling. "There you are."

"Take a seat, and we will call you when we are ready." The security guard tries to hide his terror, but his hands are shaking.

"That won't be necessary." Without another word, Vinz produces a weapon.

A cold chill shoots up Nathan's spine causing a shivering tremble throughout his body.

"Enough bells and whistles." Zayyir says, straightening up. "Let's see what this body can do."

"Don't kill him," Nathan pleads, "I never killed anyone in my life. Please, I can't live with that."

Zayyir smiles compassionately. "You don't have to live with it..."

There is movement in the lobby as security officers surround Vinz. They prepare to take him into custody. Screaming commands like, 'drop it', and 'put your hands up'.

He does none of these, he lifts the weapon and aims it at the heavy-set security guard posted behind the desk and says, "...because we are already dead."

A shot is fired. Chunks of brain surrounded by pink mist spray into the air. Soggy red tissue slaps against the wall with a moist splat.

Zayyir turns away from the observation window and takes a few steps from the door. He focuses his full attention on the physical world. With all other personas locked in the intangible prison, he has little to fear from them.

"Now," he says with a smile. "To start testing the limits of this body."

25

No one screams orders. No one fires a shot. And no one takes Vinz into custody.

Many of the people, Advancement Industries personnel of various fields, hold their heads and screech in agonizing pain. Their blood-curdling cries strike a nightmarish atmosphere throughout the lobby and the building.

Gibberish spews from their mouths. Typical office equipment becomes weapons in the hands of the infected. Any uninfected individuals find themselves overwhelmed by the sudden attack. Chaos and insanity ensue.

Vinz moves through the pandemonium with strategic precision. He lashes out with a perfect blend of gunplay and martial arts to engage those crossing his path amid the anarchy. Each movement draws him closer to the elevator.

The awful scene of blood and mayhem continues long after Vinz leaves the lobby. This is no longer a sanctuary for the technological elite. It is now ground zero for the most catastrophic event since government control faltered long ago.

With the elevator doors closing, Vinz leaves the blood bath for another tower level.

Johnny sits alone in the cell. Nathan is no longer his cellmate. He finagles with his virtual restraints. His eyes scan the walls in search of a key to his escape. In the sacred geometry that forges his surroundings, a code is required to unlock the door. He knows this because he believes this, and in that belief is the reality.

As he did in Christian Drake's mind, Johnny discovers components of his virtual bindings. He pieces them together using a computerized telepathic ability. They unite in perfect harmony.

The seemingly random lines form an image. Johnny Vinz once again sees the 'flower of life' and feels his restraints loosen before dropping off his body and falling to the floor.

Now, with the ability to move his body, Johnny peaks out of the observation window and sees Zayyir. Lost in deep concentration, his back continues to be turned to the cell.

Johnny Vinz, still being controlled by Zayyir, slaughters the last of the security agents on another level of the building on his way to the civilians who cower behind any object they can find. Most of them hide behind their desks.

He approaches a sniveling woman with her back against a corner of the room.

"This is not your fault." He says, aiming his weapon at her head. "But you are part of the problem."

The cell door unlocks, and Johnny emerges, moving quickly toward Zayyir. He places his hand on the young man's shoulder. "Hey."

Vinz' arm jerks suddenly as he pulls the trigger. The weapon blasts a slug harmlessly into the wall. With a terrified yelp, the woman sprints for safety.

Zayyir spins around to face Johnny. "Back off!" He screams with intense authority. Johnny feels the impact of an invisible force that sends him barreling back against the wall.

Security tries desperately to re-establish order in the building. Vinz stands in a momentary daze. They utilize this short-lived trance to overpower him in his moment of weakness. One of the terrified agents fires his weapon at Vinz's head. Only to miss completely as the inhuman cyborg shifts his body.

He regains his composure and slaughters every brave soul that engages him.

Once again, the doors close, containing Johnny in the elevator. Vinz waits in the metallic box, watching numbers near the ceiling indicate his ascent to Drake's office.

Zayyir is done with the peons of this company. It is time to address the source of his hatred.

Johnny and Zayyir square off against each other in the virtual arena.

"This is my mind." Zayyir snarls.

Johnny stares defiantly at the terrifying hacker. "I was here first."

The elevator doors part with a tranquil ding. As they do, the confines of Drake's office are revealed. The elderly leader of Advancement Industries sits helplessly in his chair, staring at his greatest creation. *Even Frankenstein had to face his monster.* Drake thinks. He'd been willing to sacrifice so much in the name of advancement. It was only fitting that the great Christian Drake would also have to sacrifice himself. If it came to that, he fully intended to. It would be a fitting end of his life's work.

26

"Hello." Christian Drake greets as Johnny Vinz steps out of the elevator. "With whom am I speaking?" Vinz approaches silently. "Samantha called. She said you discovered the cause of the virus."

Vinz glares at him. "It is not a virus."

Drake can do little more than stare at him from the confines of his broken body. The equipment of his chair continuously hums as they work endlessly to prohibit his frail body from fully deteriorating. His most basic body functions can no longer be left to his body.

Vinz scowls hatefully at his creator.

Drake now knows who he is speaking to. "Hello, Zayyir. Even after I rid the world of you, you are still its greatest enemy."

"Should we talk about the hundreds of thousands that you killed?" He growls.

"Nothing was ever intentional. It was in the name of advancement." Drake's computerized voice responds simply. "Besides, everyone signed a contract."

"I didn't." Vinz continues to move closer to the elderly invalid. His body shakes in random convulsions as the virtual war wages in the confines of his subconscious.

"You were a criminal."

"SO ARE YOU!!" Vinz screams so loudly he nearly damages his vocal cords. He brandishes a weapon as he nears Drake and points it at his head. "Like contracts ever mattered to you."

Drake's desk melts into the floor. He exposes his entire worthless, ALS-ridden body for Vinz to see. "I am now addressing Johnny Vinz."

"You destroyed everything!" If not for the intense conflict churning within him, tears of emotion would stream down Vinz's face. Zayyir remembers everything that this altruistic psychopath took from him. His father. His youth. His life.

"A great deal of sacrifice came with creating you and your technology. But look at the bigger picture." Drake moves his chair closer to Vinz. He can feel the cold metal press against his forehead.

Johnny holds Zayyir's face in his hands. The hacker lies on the floor with Johnny on top of him.

"No!" Zayyir screams. "This is my body!"

Johhny places his thumbs on Zayyir's eyes. "Just remember, this isn't real." He sinks his thumbs into Zayyir's eye sockets. The young hacker screeches in agonizing pain.

No longer in the confines of the technology center, Vinz feels the electrodes wiggling in his ocular cavity. He fights through the hallucinated grand mal seizure and reaches up, tearing the electrodes out of his head.

He can now see the interior of Zayyir's apartment from the confines of the liquid orb.

Vinz stumbles backward away from Drake. His hands shake violently. He shakes his head, trying to clear his mind. Unable to squeeze the trigger, Vinz tries futilely to maintain his aim.

Drake continues to stare at him. "I do not know what is going on in that brain of yours, but I want you to know I can help."

"Like you helped us before?" Vinz responds in a twisted snarl. His voice dropped to a raspy resonance.

"You are the greatest technological advancement in human history."

"I had a life!" Vinz cries out. He tries desperately to pull the trigger but is no longer in full control of his body functions. Johnny is regaining command of the body's faculties.

"So did I." Drake's eyes turn down emotionally. "This disease took everything from me.

This is what I am trying to correct." Vinz starts to lower his weapon. Small convulsions jerk the gun randomly. You are stage six. Just think of the problems we can solve. I can cure all of our biological inadequacies. Just think of-"

Johnny now stands dominantly over Zayyir. He is free of the electrodes, free of the seizure, and free of the liquid orb. Zayyir has lost nearly all control in his virtual reality.

"You want this!" He screams, "Just as much as I do!" In one last desperate motion, Zayyir reaches up and touches Johnny's eyes. "This is what they took from you."

After a sudden jolt, Johnny opens his eyes to find himself in the middle of the testing room. Unlike before, however, each chair is occupied by long-dead corpses from the experiment. Their bodies are still in the process of decomposing. Grotesque mannequins with faces twisted in frozen expressions of pain and terror. These poor souls locked in a wretched state of purgatory are the casualties of Christian Drake's ambition for progress.

Headsets cling to their decomposing skulls, refusing to release them from their hell. Light flickers from the spectacles that sit just above their eyes. Presenting images into their minds.

His attention is drawn to the twenty-third chair. The chair that held the twenty-third test subject. As he nears the eerie seat, a trembling chill crawls up his spinal cord. His body quivers from the unwanted feeling.

The decomposed carcass rejuvenates before his eyes. Horror sweeps over him, overpowering his sensibility. He stumbles slightly. The test subject is not who he thought it was. He expected to find Zayyir confined in the chair. Instead, he sees the woman from his dreams. He recognizes her. The woman with a child. The love of his life. He sees Jessica in the twenty-third chair.

She looks at him faintly and smiles. Such a tender gaze in her soft eyes. Her body is weak and broken. The sight of him feeds her exhausted body with excitement.

"It's you," Jessica says, almost unable to believe her fragile eyes.

Johnny is shocked. "You..." he clears the frog from his throat. "You're real."

Now, Johnny is no longer in the testing room. He is in a much worse place. He is back in that terrible testing area, standing in front of the fifth door. The only room without a name.

He hears the echoing voice of Jessica in the back of his mind. "Johnny." She says. "I am so sorry. I did not mean to push you away."

The medical chart still hangs next to the entrance of the room. This time, however, the name on the chart can be read. It simply reads: Johnny.

With a shaky hand, he timidly reaches for the door. It opens, and Johnny is met by a blindingly bright light. He pushes through the illumination and steps into the room.

Johnny's expression drops into a state of complete devastation. He blankly stares at Christian Drake. His eyes may be focused on the invalid, but he can only see the images inside his mind.

"-all of the diseases that I will cure. All of the technology that I will build." Drake continues to justify his actions. "After stage seven, just think of everything I will do to advance the human race. Advancement Industries will go on long after I am gone. It will go on forever."

Johnny returns completely to Drake's office. He glances at Christian Drake with the sudden realization of his personal sacrifice in this elderly man's quest for progress.

In one movement, he raises his weapon and fires a single shot. The bullet tears through Drake's fragile skull. His head explodes in an extravagant display of destruction.

The room dissolves from Drake's magnificent office to a barren room void of furniture or fixtures. Only Drake's advanced chair remains, holding the corpse in a fixed position.

Christian Drake is dead.

Johnny stares at Drake's body for a long moment. His expression is a mixture of hatred and depression. The gun hangs in his hand at his side with a light touch. He hardly has enough strength to hold the chunk of metal from falling to the floor.

He stumbles for the elevator. His feet drag against the floor.

The elevator doors part, and he unconsciously steps in.

When the doors part again, Johnny Vinz is in the Advancement Industries lobby. A slew of security personnel surround the elevator. The chaotic catastrophe has subsided. No longer plagued by the insane actions of the infected, the security forces focus their full attention on Johnny Vinz. Many of their hands shake with fear and adrenaline.

"Drop the weapon and lay on the ground. NOW!!" One of the military police orders. They do not expect him to do this. They know the deal. This is the moment that an infected person, confronted by a superior force, commits suicide. Their bodies reanimate in a terrible display of violence. This does not happen, however.

"He said drop it!" Another voice screams.

Johnny slowly drops the weapon as he emerges from the elevator into the lobby. Confusion sweeps over everyone in the half-circle surrounding the elevator. Johnny kneels on the ground and places his hands behind his head.

The entire security force is baffled. Their expectations were dashed by a display of humble surrender.

"He's not killing himself?" One of the security agents asks, turning to his fellow officers.

"Isn't he infected?" Another voice questions.

"What do we do?"

They all stare apprehensively, and Johnny Vinz is even more scared than they were with the expectation of suicidal homicide.

He waits patiently as the security force takes him into custody. His work is done.

27

A recording is played. This audio and video documentation is the accumulated report of the recent events. The sound of an investigator's haggard voice starts the report.

He reads his findings. "Suspect identified as Johnny Vinz. He is being held in cell twelve pending further psychological assessment. Traces of the Mayhem Virus are still detected, which could explain his inability to recognize his own name. It is unclear whether he remembers killing one hundred twenty-three people before being captured. The following video was exported from his brain augmentation. Please note that there is no evidence of the incident."

CONNECTING .... COMPLETE
ANALYZING.................... COMPLETE
SYNCHRONIZING............ COMPLETE
ACTIVATING...
3..
2..
1..

^)(*&#^^K*R$^(*YY%^!#@However I feel it is my obligation#E^%^jui(*%$%595F*/(frgrf....

ADJUSTING...

%&(#$!@)$&#=$%^8!

ADJUSTING...

iImMEeODJA;C A98SOKEJthose

ADJUSTING...

can't see. I wonder how long I'll bee her. I can't believe I even got here. I didn't do anything.

I wasn't even there. Was I! I Was? I didn't mean, not me /killedd I me90151$%

ADJUSTING...

bUT today was a good Day I, didn't catch any Viruses and I'm happy but I don't know when they were going to let me go cause I was promised to go if i...iF

I...hope I don't get a shot today* This shouldn't be hear. I think I've doing a good job in Page 12 done evertying they ask I just hope that they will reword me for it by offering me freedomination.

Been sick most the day. Probably the food they made me eat. It doesn't even look like food anymore. I wonder if anyone else gets the same food? I wonder if there are anyone else!

Not long ago I heard crying closer than I heard before. They don't let me see anyone but the doctors. Maybe this is illegal and they can't do this because it is wrong and if it was wrong then why can they do it? Every time a gun is fired a junky dies in the streets.

Wow, my little brother told me that when I was a kid.

Why am I thinking about that now? It doesn't make sense. I wonder what they're doing to me? Am I awake? Can I get up? Why can't I move? I wonder if they give me a sedative of something that makes me not move!

I wonder if they read my letter: Not the document that they made me sign before I did this. I remember that one it was the one that said that I give my consent that they do whatever experiment they need to do to see if my brain does what it is supposed to do with what they gave me. That I will undergo a lot of conditioning in preparation for this experiment including but not restricted to eating specific food, taking their medication, watching their programs. I have willingly participated in experiments but still haven't seen, I cant' wait to get back to my sell and read my letter. I've read it so many times I don't know if I even need to read the test anymore because I have memorized so much answers. I have memorized everything I have seen lately. It never changes. I see the same paper everyday. I don't have many choices, either I speak the costumer copy of the document or I can eat the letter from Mimi.

I love my daughter/hope she healthy cause important I remember when I took her to the circus. I didn't know before then that she was afraid of clowns. I wonder if she knew that and didn't tell me. I wondered that the whole ride home. I haven't seen her since she was four. I wonder if she would still be afraid of clowns.

Why didn't she come to visit me? Did she? and they just didn't let her see me because they wanted me to sign the document? I think so because she said she would visit me when she got a chance. My Page 1 god, she is at least 20 years old. Where has my life gone? How did I get here? So many mistakes that I thought I could have made better decisions, what was wrong with me to make so many stupid decisions! I should have spoken to a judge before signing then I would know when they would let me go. (=+*#% I hear that @#^$*&) what is.....^$&..

ADJUSTING...

I'm still waiting for people waiting for people waiting .... still can't find the beginning of the circle. It doesn't lose sense. I can't think because it doesn't make any sense to think....that....that....voice doesn't belong. Something I can't see is in my M-MM-BRAIN. I've got to go soon, I will be late for school and I don't know my name.

Can't think I thought that. But no matter how hard I try I still think that^s not right at all.

This feels funny@ the lunatic. Could you see the smile on faces of parents because their children make good for image of public people jo. I need to find a TV television# And pa9oi thought;;so can't dsaoijghwe8ye944

ERROR

CAN'[T do I se*e ai#
ophg94$@#oigry!p5%&98&%^74

ADJUSTING

ERROR

$$$

ERROR

That voice is I can't...I feel it but

I can't;adofi*ao438aorie;h#$8a;gnvdk%lcmx, dsg~`aklnrtio<q4hoagjvsdkn'dpbhgu7?>eitbj$$$ k.4 mkqrmgaibsj(

FATAL ERROR

ochvuGbshf.jtnkmgjabisHVDUb.kjtq/ gwlknasijbz

9ucSVDHejf/lkngaoijdsvOhnkltm2jogwpadu9s vaht2/lknjigweaueoijt jewguv8/lkn5r3i

2ewfyhlkn/t32r wefhub.jt3rk 2fh jtr23ewfhB

CONNECTION LOSS...

A security camera records two people in a single room. Johnny Vinz sits in an isolated cell of a maximum-security building. He sits with a blank expression on his face. His arms and legs are securely bound to the metalic chair.

Across from him, a psychological analyst shuffles through her notes. She twirls a pen in her fingers. "I've been asked to consult on your evaluation."

She glances up at him. He does not return her gaze. Instead, his eyes stare blankly at a spot on the floor. A small dribble of drool suspends from his mouth, seeking to break itself from his lips and fall to the ground. He does not notice this. He does not notice anything. He is catatonic.

"Do you know where you are?" The doctor asks as her eyes return to her paperwork. These are preestablished questions designed to invoke a response. She cannot assess him if he does not respond. "Do you know what you did?" There is a slight flutter of frustration.

This is her job, and she does it well, but she is still human. The horrific actions committed by this individual recently make her feel resentment deep within her bones. She wants nothing more than to prove that he deserves to be executed. Though, part of her believes this will happen regardless of her assessment.

"Do you remember your name? Can you tell me your name?"

Words ooze out of his mouth. "They call me Johnny Vinz. But that is not my name."

Her eyes gaze upward in surprise. This is the first time he has spoken since being taken into custody. "It's not? Why do you say that? Who are you?" *Is this a split personality situation? Is he lost in psychosis?* She is genuinely curious.

Johnny Vinz slowly lifts his head. His eyes set on the doctor with a dazed gaze. "Johnny Vinz is the name of dead men."

The doctor continues to scribble in her notes. Her eyes move between her paperwork and her patient. "How did they die? Who are they?"

"Casualties of progress," Vinz responds with a slight smirk.

More notes are scribbled. The movement of the pain picks up pace with concern and intrigue. "Who were these people before they became casualties?"

His persona changes. His body straightens into a rigged posture. An expression of a hardened military soldier hardens his face. "Victor was a soldier. He believed in the cause. He volunteered for the mission. It is what he was made for."

Dropping from the structured pose of a soldier, Johnny Vinz wiggles into a feminine form. "Innessa was a spy. She listened to the wrong people. She took the wrong job. She learned too much to live but was too valuable to die."

Sadness sweeps over him. No longer expressing femininity, his gaze turns back to the ground in depression. "Nathan the professor. He solved their problem. People win awards for what he did, but he was killed for it."

The doctor continues to scribble her notes. She feels a strange energy coming from Johnny Vinz. He stares at her with burning intensity. "Zayyir, the hacker, discovered what they were doing. He knew that a child could not go to war with a corporation. He knew they would do what they chose to do, regardless of any moral, ethical, or populace objections. But he also knew that everything they did was under the cover of darkness. They hid their actions behind confusion and isolation. He believed that if their actions were exposed, people would turn away from them. Without the pristine facade of perfection, they would be forced to abandon their disgraceful ambition. He was wrong."

She tries not to show any emotions. As with many others, she's heard about the great and terrible hacker Zayyir. His infamy runs deep in the underbelly of society. She never thought that hearing his name would bring her fear. But it does.

"If they are just dead people," she begins her next question, "then what is your name?"

Johnny Vinz leans back in a persona completely unique to those that he just portrayed. "They call me Johnny Vinz. Our name is Subject Six."

The video feed cuts out and the investigator's voice returns with the same overworked tone.

"Under corporate order nine, two, four three, suspect is hereby remanded to highest level of isolation. No network connection and minimal physical contact will be allowed. Suspects augmentations are to be considered weapons of mass destruction. This ends the assessment."

THE END

Printed in the USA
CPSIA information can be obtained
at www.ICGtesting.com
LVHW021934150924
790970LV00008B/295/J

9 798868 500466